Shadows

of the

Heart

Shadows

of the

Heart

PATTY G. HENDERSON

BLANCA ROSA Publishing

2014

SHADOWS OF THE HEART

Copyright © 2014 Patty G. Henderson
Published by Blanca Rosa Publishing
All Rights Reserved
ISBN: 978-0-692-29641-7

This book is a work of fiction. Names, characters, places, and incidents are a product of the author's imagination or are used fictitiously. Any resemblance to actual events, locales, or persons, living or dead, is coincidental.

Book Cover: Boulevard Photografica/Patty G. Henderson
www.boulevardphotografica.yolasite.com

"...to your shadow, will I make true love."

SHAKESPEARE *Two Gentlemen of Verona*
(1623) IV. ii. 121

Thank You Notes

As I writer, I've noticed something over the past 9 novels that I've written: Some books are easier than others to write and to edit. It's one of the mysteries of the writing process that can inspire and frustrate—sometimes simultaneously! Who knows why, but it is a fact.

If SHADOWS OF THE HEART is a good read and a good book, I have some special people to thank.

My undying Thanks and Gratitude I forever shower to my Muse, my most ardent supporter and dearest friend, T.T. Thomas. Thank you, Tarra, always. To Terry Baker and Jean Baker, my dear friends from across the pond, and to my writing friends, Marsha A. Moore and Juli D. Revezzo, my fellow Writing Ladies, who keep me energized and believing in the magic of writing, and a shout out to Jackie Maestas of Lavender Dragon Edit, for help with some of the proofing.

And always, always, I love you, Mama. You went away to be with the Lord on October 5th, 2010, but forever remain the wind beneath my wings.

Patty G. Henderson
September, 2014

One

The March afternoon was cooler than the normal chill for the time of year. Mr. Augustus Taylor did not help the matter. Mr. Taylor, his wife and I were in the living room of his sister, Mrs. Sarah Bentley, where I had lived in her service as companion for the last two years.

He'd motioned me to a well worn chair too near a drafty window. He rocked slightly on his heels as he stood directly in front of the fireplace, blocking the solitary source of heat in the room. The small amount of warmth from the candles was sucked up by the three of us occupying the relatively small space. How far I had fallen from being the pampered child of a wealthy man! Would life ever get any better for me?

Mr. Taylor cleared his throat for the second time. He seemed stiff and unsure of how to begin.

"I remind you, Miss Stewart, that although I am under no obligation to be concerned about your future, since there are no ties of blood that bind us, I am nonetheless a man of principle. I will not see an unprotected young lady thrown out upon the world, bereft of resources. The care you afforded my sister was more than adequate, and she grew quite fond of you. Therefore..."

He paused, and Mrs. Taylor, the other in the room stealing my warmth, interrupted.

"Indeed. It was a fortunate chance, you see, that Lady Blackstone should be in need of a companion and that it came to our attention."

"Winifred, allow me to proceed with Miss Stewart," Mr. Taylor said irritably. He turned back to me. "Mrs. Taylor is correct. It is within my power to recommend you for the position, Miss Stewart. I'm to assume you will have heard of the Blackstones?"

I looked at him squarely. Was it to be my lot to be handed down from wealthy family to wealthy family, like a lamp or piece of furniture?

"I believe your sister spoke of them briefly," I answered in a low tone. I could not feign interest. I lacked that talent.

"Indeed," continued Mr. Taylor, "the present Lord Blackstone succeeded the earldom upon the death of his father, Laurence Blackstone, five years ago. Last spring, he married Lenore Marie LaSalle, at which time his mother decided to return to the Dowager House with her younger daughter, Mistress Victoria Blackstone."

I knew the story from here. No doubt, the old lady Blackstone needed another nursemaid or companion to clean up after and nurse her.

"And is it the Dowager Lady Blackstone who is need of a companion?"

"Oh, dear no," said Mrs. Taylor hastily. "It's the young Lady Blackstone. She is a sweet girl, barely twenty one, but her spirits are in a dark spiral. She was shattered when she found out some months back that she had no hopes of giving the Earl an heir." Mrs. Taylor, a rotund woman with large, red cheeks, leaned forward in her chair and spoke quietly. "She lost her first pregnancy and the news from the doctors was bad. She can bear no more children. The Earl is frequently in London for long periods and the doctors believe companionship, someone close to the Lady's own age could be very beneficial to lifting her spirits."

I smiled, my own spirits brightening. At last, I no longer needed to worry about grumpy old women who could not help themselves and complained constantly about youth. This could be a very different and more uplifting turn in my life.

"It was very kind of you to think of me, Mr. and Mrs. Taylor," I said, truly grateful.

He puffed his chest out. "The care you gave to my sister in her final years makes you more than eligible for the position. If you are agreeable, I can speak to the Dowager Lady Blackstone on your behalf as soon as I return home. I'm certain you should have no worries about obtaining the position. I daresay the Dowager has every confidence in my judgment."

"She has indeed, Augustus." Mrs. Taylor nodded. She was more like a brown mouse of a woman who echoed words of praise to each breath her husband exhaled. "And in the meantime, Augustus, I don't think there could be objection to Miss Stewart remaining here until she leaves for Blackstone Castle." She cast a look at her husband.

"Oh, none at all, of course," he affirmed. "No doubt she can be useful in helping the servants with the inventory of china and such which we are having conveyed to the Grange."

So, my life was neatly arranged. I could utter no objections. I had none. And I had no alternatives either. At the very least, I would get more restful sleep, assured that my immediate future was provided for. Three years ago, my future was brilliant, my prospects glowing. But that was before my father shot himself. I resented him for that. Yes, resented him. He never told me. Never talked to me or confided the futility he must have felt in his life. Was I not his only daughter? Did I not count in his heart? I hadn't understood then and still don't.

He could have explained that he had gambled our entire fortune away. And we'd had a fortune. I loved being part of the wealthy circle. I loved my father and our life. But my world shattered into tiny, bitter fragments of angry memories. That is all I had left. There was no family that I could turn to. In the end, my godmother, old Mrs. Bentley, had grudgingly opened the door to her home in the tall house in Bath, where I lived the life of drudgery: fetching, carrying about and exercising a snotty, wheezing bulldog and looking after the library and playing endless games of piquet with Mrs. Bentley.

That was until four days ago, when she succumbed to an apoplectic seizure and died where she sat. It was unfortunate, but Mrs. Bentley had been an enormous woman who never cared about the excess of food and wine and the effects they might have on her health. She lost all control once Mr. Bentley passed away.

I was certain to once again be homeless and penniless. 'Twas a good thing I had learned to foster a good personality and attitude, for to find oneself in such an unenviable position for the second time surely would have driven most young ladies of twenty-two nearly mad, especially one reared to the life of ease and comfort. No, I was no weakling, despite my delicate looks once compared to "Dresden China." In the years following my father's death, I had to toughen my outer shell and my inner soul. It hadn't been easy. I'd been carefree and loved openly and freely. Now, I guarded my heart under lock and key. I gave my all to service but that was all I gave.

Two

I busied myself washing and wrapping fragile glass and china and packing in shavings. I had a restful night's sleep to more fully appreciate my new predicament. The Lady Blackstone was young. That would be a totally new experience for me, one I was genuinely grateful to Mr. Taylor for his efforts on my behalf. In this second decade of the nineteenth century, there were no avenues open for an unmarried, penniless ex-gentlewoman to earn her keep except as a governess or a companion. I wasn't particularly good at or enamored of either options, but there were no others and I could not be choosey.

Indeed, I found myself quite looking forward to be going to Blackstone Castle in service to Lady Blackstone. Mrs. Bentley had been too old. She'd completely forgotten what it was like to be young. There were times when I thought I would simply wither away in the dark corridors of the old house. I suffered with nightmares, waking up thinking I was gray and shriveled as Mrs. Bentley!

Mr. Taylor was as good on his word. Within a week, I had been summoned to Blackstone Castle. Instructions came that I was to take the Bath stage coach to Lustleigh, a small township in Devon and wait at the only inn where a conveyance from Blackstone Castle would meet me. The castle itself lay atop a high cliff near the bogs and moors of Dartmoor. I must say, I could not suppress a shiver, for I had heard of the forsaken land in Dartmoor. The salary proposed, while not anywhere near what father bestowed on me as pin money, nonetheless, was quite an attractive sum considering my Godmother, Mrs. Bentley, had paid me nothing. I was lucky for room and board and food and clothing, she once said with a stern look and voice. This smelled of freedom to me. I would be working for wages and not charity.

And so it was that I bade farewell without regret, I must say, to the dark and drafty house in Bath. Instead, I found myself in the medium-sized, well worn coach along rough country roads, heading to even more brutal land and Devon, my entire earthly possessions in corded luggage atop the coach. I had donned a sober-colored grey pelisse over a black dress, with a plain black bonnet. In no uncertain terms, Mrs. Bentley had sharply informed me that a girl in my position should never be conspicuous. I should never wear my hair down, only in private. So, I had pulled my blond hair tightly away from my face. Nevertheless, tiny wisps of hair trailed down the back of the bonnet. Mrs. Bentley had been only too aware of the stares I gathered from the young men when I went for shopping. She needn't have worried.

If only she'd known that I cared not for the young men. I eyed the young ladies instead. I could not speak of this, of course, for it certainly would have cost me to be kicked out into the streets, too tarnished for anyone to give me work or take me in. I knew I would never marry, unless by happenstance, I could make prior arrangements with a suitor who might share my interest in others of his same sex. Merely a dream, I knew, but I had to keep some dreams alive.

It was near dark when we finally reached Lustleigh. I ached from the long and bumpy coach ride. Cold and stiff, I reveled in the thought of the coffee-room fire at the inn, but I had little money with me to spare and besides, the carriage from Blackstone Castle could already be waiting.

The coachman heaved my luggage down to the cobblestones, took the few coins I handed him and disappeared into the inn, leaving me alone. I cast a look toward the narrow road that continued up toward the hills of Dartmoor. I was lucky. I didn't have long to wait. A smart looking gig came into view from the near darkness and pulled up directly before me. The groom, dressed in brown with black boots and hat, jumped down and came toward me.

"Might you be Miss Annalee Stewart, Miss?" He seemed cheerful enough.

"Yes, I am Miss Stewart."

He tipped his hat and without another word, hoisted my luggage atop his shoulders. I followed him with a brisk step.

Inside the coach, there was a thick blanket lying on the leather seat. I was thankful for it, for the nightfall had brought a slight chill to the air. I placed the blanket over my lap and settled in.

I took the opportunity to ask the young groom how much further to the castle.

"Not far to the lodge gate, Miss, but the drive up to the actual castle is all of a mile. The trip is too long for her Ladyship these days so she rarely comes to the village on account of her health."

I was beside myself to learn all I could of the Blackstones, but I didn't think it would be at all proper to question a servant about his employers. It was unthinkable. I would simply have to wait and batten down all the butterflies in a flurry in my stomach. Time enough to find out all I wanted, or not, of the Blackstones.

Three

As the coach made its way through thick, wild forest land, I sat silent and apprehensive in the seat. We were rushing ever closer to Blackstone Castle. I could feel it. The trees the rig squeezed by were giant, brooding and nearly suffocated the narrow road.

We cleared the cramped woods onto a long road that led up higher into a steep cliff path lined with a brown wooden fence. Beyond, I could hear the hard rush of water below.

We finally reached what the groom had called "the lodge gate" and the lodge gate keeper swung them open to allow our gig to pass through. The keeper cast a curious glance my way. I looked down to avoid his intrusive stare. The coach trundled on as the road wound higher and higher up the cliff side.

Suddenly, the sound of a horse's hoofs startled me, and a solitary rider rounded the curve of the path, coming toward us at a pace that suggested the hounds of hell might be at his heels. I leaned partly out the window to take a closer look at the rider. It was a woman, her loose dark hair flying behind her! In seconds, she was past us at a thundering gallop, not even stopping. I followed her and gasped.

"Who on earth was that?"

The groom looked down at me and grinned. "That was Wild Torrie. Always rides at a wicked pace, she does, when she's coming from the castle. She's happy to get it behind her, I imagine."

"Wild Torrie?" I asked, intrigued. What kind of name was that? "But she was wearing breeches and—"

"Not meaning any disrespect, Miss," the groom said awkwardly. "It's just the name they've given her in the village on account of her...different ways. She's his Lordship's sister, Miss Victoria Blackstone."

"Oh," I said, sitting back in my seat. I tried to remember what Mr. Taylor had said. But I never expected a woman to behave so outrageously. She was riding that horse like a man. What kind of lady did that? "She lives with her mother in the Dower House, does she not?" I asked, the image of the woman with the wild, dark burgundy hair still alive in my mind.

"Yes, Miss," the groom boomed loudly from his perch. "It's over beyond the trees ahead." He pointed to the right.

We continued up the road until again, the thoughts of apprehension gripped me. What kind of people were the Blackstones? Would my life go from tolerable to worse? I had vowed to always improve my lot in life as I moved forward. I never wanted to look back or to take a step backwards again. What kept me strong and courageous was the belief that one day, I would have everything I had grown accustomed to in my childhood. A beautiful home all my own and someone to share it with--Someone strong and with equally strong beliefs in morals that I held sacred in my own life. Someone unlike my father.

Suddenly, the road leveled off and in the distance, the castle stood before me towering atop the cliff. It was an intimidating pile, silhouetted against the deepening early dusky sky. I held my breath. I could not deny that it held a foreboding air.

As the coach continued the approach to Blackstone Castle, I could not help notice the large cannons flanking the arched gateway. They were huge. There was a courtyard beyond the gate and beyond the walls, the ground fell steeply to the river below. I wrapped my arms around myself as I could not control the cold chill that went through me.

The groom brought the gig to a halt right before an oversized, heavily studded oak door. Jumping from his driver's perch, he opened the carriage door, offered his hand and escorted me out. With the wave of one hand, he pointed toward the giant oak door and then turned abruptly and began taking my luggage from atop the coach.

Part of me wanted to stay put and not move an inch toward the foreboding door, but the part of me that had learned to survive and scrape for every meager little thing I owned pushed me forward. I walked slowly and pulled the bell hanging on the door. It suddenly opened immediately, so sudden that I stepped back, startled. My tongue tied, I tried to sound intelligent to the butler who stood staring stiffly, waiting for me.

"I...I'm Miss Annalee Stewart. Lady Blackstone is expecting me."

He nodded slowly. "I shall inform the housekeeper of your arrival, Miss Stewart," he said with a haughty voice.

He was a bland man, who seemed stuck in all the etiquette and expectations of his station. Brown hair, brown eyes and pale skin. The poor man must not spend much time outdoors.

I followed him, glancing back at the groom and wondering who would take care of my belongings. We went through an enormous hall, the ceiling lost in the darkness and the stone floor so cold that I thought I could feel the cold right through my worn shoes. The walls were rich in paneled oak and a log fire flickered within the hearth of an intricately carved stone mantle. My gaze caught the collection of ancient weapons hanging above the fireplace. To our right was a broad staircase that led up to the gallery. I could not help but admire and marvel at the faded magnificence of Blackstone Castle.

From the darkening hallway, the housekeeper appeared. She seemed a dignified woman, dressed in black bombazine with a chatelaine of keys belted at her waist.

She looked at me with interest. "I'm Mrs. Patterson, the housekeeper, Miss. Her ladyship is currently resting, and her instructions were that I should show you to your rooms and that you were to wait her summons there. Will you come this way, Miss Stewart?"

Without waiting for my response, she turned and headed for the staircase. I had to hurry to follow her. She moved at a brisk pace. As we reached the top of the gallery, one of the doors lining the long hallway opened suddenly and a woman stood framed in the doorway. I barely got a look at her before she quickly stepped back and closed the door behind her. Who else lived at Blackstone, I wondered.

We continued down the corridor until Mrs. Patterson stopped at the very end and opened the door to a room on the left. She stood stone-faced and pointed.

"This is to be your room, Miss."

The bedchamber I entered was darkly paneled and the heavy, deep red brocade curtains and hangings on the four poster bed did nothing to brighten the room. But who was I to complain? The room was richly furnished with expensive, if slightly used furnishings. This room, in fact, was superior to anything I'd had at Mrs. Bentley's house. I would need to learn to be more thankful and less critical.

"I will have your belongings sent up, and Betsy shall bring some hot water for wash up," said Mrs. Patterson. "Being that his Lordship is away, her Ladyship will be dining in her sitting room instead of the dining room. I'll have your supper sent up to you late."

"Thank you, Mrs. Patterson," I said, hoping that the tray would be adequate to quiet my increasingly grumbling stomach. I hadn't eaten since the morning before leaving Bath.

I'd barely taken off my bonnet and pelisse and straightened my straggling loose hairs, when a young man staggered in with my luggage, placing the three pieces haphazardly on the floor. And right behind him, a young lady I assumed to be Betsy, followed with a jug of hot water. She was a fresh-faced girl with a pleasant, round face. I smiled at her.

"Good evening," I said. "You must be Betsy? I'm Miss Stewart."

The young girl smiled wide, but her gaze mostly remained down. "Yes, Miss, Betsy. Mrs. Patterson said I was to tell you to ring when you're ready and I'll be the one taking you to her Ladyship. She's woke now and asking to see you."

"Thank you, Betsy." I smiled at her again. I could get used to being here at Blackstone Castle. So far, the special treatment I was getting was heavenly. I had to be careful not to get too spoiled. It would not be like this everywhere and I had learned never to take anything for granted. How long would this last? Would I hit it off with Lady Blackstone? I simply had to make it work. Where else would I go? I could be cleaning kettles and dishes at some Godforsaken inn in the middle of nowhere. For how long would Blackstone Castle be my home?

Four

I washed quickly, changed my traveling dress for a blue merino which was only slightly less shabby than my old black one and rang the bell. I was excited yet apprehensive to meet Lady Lenore Blackstone.

To my surprise, Betsy answered promptly, holding the door open for me. As we both walked briskly along the corridor, the same door as before opened and the same woman appeared. Only this time, she didn't shy away into her room.

"Ah, Betsy," she said in a somewhat serious tone, "I shall take Miss Stewart to her Ladyship. You may go about your duties now."

"Yes, Miss Drake," Betsy said with a hasty courtesy and sped away into the shadowy corridor, leaving me in the charge of the mysterious other woman. I finally saw that she was a plump, short woman with intruding wisps of gray hair sprinkled in the dark brown. She eyed me from head to shoes, not a smile on her face. I must admit, I rather objected to her intrusive glare.

"I am her Ladyship's personal maid. I'm Miss Drake." She was ice cold. I didn't like her sly way of looking up under her lashes. I found her uncomfortable. Her voice didn't sound extremely educated, yet she didn't have the rough, country accent of Betsy either. I prided myself in being an excellent judge of character. I had been forced to hone my instincts to a sharp edge since having to fend for myself. If I was to be bounced around from household to household, I knew I had to gather my wits and skills of character assessment. So it startled me to sense such strong antipathy from this stranger, Miss Drake, and I towards her.

"Good evening, Miss Drake." I smiled as pleasantly as I could muster.

The woman did not respond to my overture, but instead gave me only a nod, and with downcast eyes, glided ahead.

"Her Ladyship's suite is just further along this way," she said, as she walked past the head of the staircase, to the end of the gallery, opposite my own rooms. Miss Drake knocked before opening, and led me into a sitting room which was thick with the color rose. It added an unnatural glow to the whole room. Rose colored silk drapes hung along the large windows and an oversized Aubusson carpet lay in the middle of the enormous room.

On a daybed, pulled up close to the fireplace, lay a young woman wrapped in lilac robes. She raised herself on one elbow as Miss Drake and I entered.

"Miss Stewart, my Lady," Miss Drake announced.

"Oh, pray, come in Miss Stewart," Lady Blackstone said in a nervous voice. "Thank you, Miss Drake. That will be all."

As I approached her, I could not help but notice the woman's startling look of fragility. Her skin was unnaturally pale, her frame too thin beneath all the volume of robes wrapped about her. But despite the waif appearance, I was taken by the lustrous, golden wavy hair which draped loose to her shoulders and the wide, child-like blue eyes which gazed at me intently. How old was Lenore Blackstone, really? In spite of the difference in the social status and the fact that I was told there was only a few years difference in age between us, I felt immeasurably older and healthier than this lovely woman before me.

"You are so young," exclaimed Lady Blackstone ingeniously. "I mean to say, I knew you were to be young, but I had expected you to be grim and poker-faced!" She laughed, her large eyes twinkling. "I am so glad that you are not any of those things."

"So am I." I could not suppress a wide smile. "To be honest, Lady Blackstone, I wondered at my last job, that perhaps my life as a companion might not just cause me to wither away. Now, I am reassured that I have indeed not died on the vine after all." I felt very much at ease with her and hoped and prayed I had not been too open in greeting her.

Her brows creased. "Is it horrid then, being a companion? I don't think I should make a good one myself, for I am too dense. People often tell me so."

"Companions are not required to be clever," I said, "merely good at tending to pet dogs, reading aloud and playing cards." I could not take my gaze from her big, blue eyes.

"Did you do all those things for Mrs. Bentley, then? Well, matters not, you shall not have to do them here, for I have no pet dog, though I think I might like a spaniel. I do very little reading and I detest cards." She laughed again, a sweet, light laughter. "In fact, Miss Stewart, I cannot conceive what you will find to do, for I am not active as I was. I find it difficult to handle much exertion."

I did wonder about the Lady Blackstone's condition and found it perplexing. I had not been told that the Lady was near infirm. Low spirits is one thing, but bed-ridden is another. What was really wrong with Lady Blackstone? While I wanted to know, I was just hired. It was not my position to ask such personal and impertinent questions. For now.

"But surely, my Lady, now with nice warmer weather coming, you will want to go strolling on the grounds, or going out to visit your friends."

The Lady shook her head ever so lightly. "I haven't many friends, you see. I could visit my mother-in-law, of course, but she does lose her patience with me sometimes." She let out a low sigh and cast her stunning blue eyes down. "I have tried to be a good and proper wife to Foster, but I had no notion that marriage was...that marriage was going to be like this. And now that I have failed miserably to give my husband a child, my fate is dismal, I fear." Her mouth quivered and her eyes filled with tears.

I was shocked and surprised at her frankness to a total stranger. "But surely, you both have plenty of time for that. To try again, I mean, your Ladyship." I added quickly.

She never removed her gaze from me, a wistful look upon her face. "Foster is scarcely here. I think he purposely avoids me now. His mother, the Dowager, blames me for that." She smiled. "And I am not sure I miss him at all." She finished her last words in a whisper.

I bit my lip to remind myself to think before I spoke. I found it most unfitting that my young and attractive employer, the Lady Blackstone, should confide in me in such detail and personal delicate matters. What was I to do? I thought that perhaps the Lady had been in dire need of someone to confide in and if talking to me could help her regain her spirits, then surely, I could encourage her, for as long as I kept the confidence and not betrayed her, then no harm be done.

But what exactly was wrong with Lady Blackstone? Perhaps with more time gone by, I could inquire of the Lady herself. There was more to Blackstone Castle and the Lady Blackstone herself. It wasn't something out in the open. No, this hid in the shadows, away from prying eyes and curiosity. I just had to look in the right places and gain the trust of the right people.

Five

A knock on the door interrupted my thoughts. A footman carrying a large tray with covered dishes entered the room. He pulled up a small table to the edge of the day bed.

It was time for me to go so as to allow her privacy for supper.

"If you'll excuse me, Lady Blackstone, but Mrs. Patterson said she would have a tray sent to my own room. I should leave."

"Oh, no. Please, won't you stay and eat your dinner here," the Lady urged eagerly. "I do so dislike dining alone." She looked at the footman who stood waiting to be dismissed. "Gerald, tell Mrs. Patterson to give you Miss Stewart's tray and bring it in here. We shall be dining together." Her smile was sweet.

"Very good, my Lady," answered Gerald passively.

It wasn't long before I was partaking of the best and most scrumptious meal I'd had in years, well, since before my father gambled all our fortune away, anyway. The delicately baked carp was divine, but it paled compared to the fricassee of veal. My admiration of Mrs. Patterson's culinary skills grew enormously. The woman could cook.

As exquisite as the main meal was, Lenore Blackstone merely pecked at her food, pushing her plate away after taking only a couple mouthfuls of the delicious offering. She washed it down with a sip of red wine. If I hadn't been so sated, it would not have been below my self-esteem to offer to finish off what she had left.

She eyed me with a keen curiosity. I almost felt shy under her intense gaze.

"I wish I could feel hungry like you," she finally murmured wistfully, "but my head aches terribly and Doctor Llewellyn's drops only cause me to fall into a light sleep."

"Then why take them before supper, my Lady?" Why not after you've eaten so you can have enough food?" It was only the sensible thing to do, I thought.

"Do you ever suffer from headaches, Miss Stewart?"

I was fortunate. I was as healthy as a working girl could be. Heaven knew I had enough reason for headaches. Lots of them. But I could not allow headaches or other ills to cause me to be bed-bound. If I were confined to a bed, I could not work. If I didn't work, I would starve.

"Only rarely," I said. "Lady Blackstone, I am certain that plenty of sunshine and walks will go a long way to getting rid of your headaches. But if your head aches now, would you like me to bathe your forehead with Hungary Water?"

"If you wish," sighed Lady Blackstone, sinking back into her pillow.

I always traveled with Hungary Water. It offered me great relief in times of stress and worry. At times, when I felt faint, the water brought me about to function. And Mrs. Bentley, during her last days, had grown obsessed with her misplaced belief in its healing powers.

I took the brown flask containing the water from my reticule and poured some gently onto a linen handkerchief. I placed it softly upon the Lady's brow. Her eyelids fluttered and she murmured softly.

"That feels so blessedly cool and you have such a gentle touch. Not at all like Miss Drake. Her hands are hard and she hurts me."

On purpose? I could not help to be concerned over the Lady's admission. I had to admit that I was ashamed how ready I was to believe ill of that bitter, somber woman, Miss Drake. Why did I have such a visceral rejection of the personal maid? Could her dark mood be affecting Lady Blackstone's recovery?

"Oh, my head feels so much better now, Miss Stewart," the frail Lady said with renewed energy. "What is your given name, Miss Stewart?" She was looking at me with a relaxed gaze.

I cleared my throat. The easy familiarity came as a surprise. "Annalee."

Lady Blackstone smiled, her blue eyes sparkling. "Well, mine is Lenore. I would like it if you could call me by my name as if we were not employer and staff." She smiled warmly. "I have a feeling we will be more than just that." Her smile did not falter. "Yes, Annalee, you must call me Lenore."

Inside, I trembled. Once I got past the shock, another warmer glow seemed to settle within my heart. I lowered my gaze, so as not to reveal my excitement. I could hardly speak properly.

"I hardly expect Lord Blackstone or the Dowager Lady Blackstone would approve," I reminded her gently. What else could I say? My heart was pounding like a swift race horse. I struggled to understand why this woman, a Lady in the highest sense of the phrase, would wish to be so...familiar...with me.

Lenore sat up, excited. "Well, we shall not do it in their presence, of course. It will be our own little secret." Her hand reached out and took hold of mine. Too quick for me to withdraw. A hot shiver of...something...went through me. Lenore's hand was so chilled to the touch. But it wasn't a cold chill that I felt. No, most assuredly it was hot and electric.

"Now that we have met," continued Lenore, "I know I shall love having a companion. I languish while Foster..." she paused. "Foster is Lord Blackstone. Well, while Foster is away, I never have anyone to talk to or share secrets with or take walks with but Miss Drake, and I am not at ease with her." She stopped and shook her head of golden tresses, a crease at her brows. "She looks at me in such a queer way."

"Why have you not dismissed her, then?" I blurted out before even thinking. Here I was, just newly hired, and being so bold as to advise the Lady of the House on her own personal matters.

Lenore shook her head. "Foster has forbidden me to do so. He says the Drake family has always served the Blackstones. She has a brother who is a gamekeeper here and she, at one time, was employed at the castle nurseries

24

until my mother-in-law had her trained as a personal maid. Miss Drake is so devoted to Foster that she refused to go to the Dower House with the Dowager. So, he made the decision that she should stay here and attend to me instead."

"I see." Obviously, this beautiful woman was submissive to a domineering Lord. Not uncommon among the aristocracy.

The footman, Gerald, came back and removed the food trays. Not a moment later, Miss Drake appeared. Thoroughly ignoring my presence, she addressed Lenore.

"Are you ready to retire, my Lady?"

Lenore cast a disappointed gaze my way and then looked at Miss Drake.

"If I must, I suppose so," she sighed wearily. She cast her look back to me.

"Miss Stewart, I will see you in the morning. Will you come for me after breakfast?" Her big blue eyes stared eagerly at me.

"You have my word, Lady Blackstone," I said properly and smiled. "Good night, my Lady." I turned and left the room without a word to the snobbish personal maid.

I cared not that I had ignored Miss Drake. It was tit for tat, I say. I allowed myself a tiny smile of revenge. I continued down the hallway toward my own room.

I was certain it was not my own imagination. Miss Drake's enmity was bold and in my face. I continued, however, to be dismayed by that and also startled at my own similar feelings toward her. It had been an almost instant impression. I had no fears that the maid could turn Lenore against me. No, what worried me more was how little authority Lenore Blackstone had in her own household. And what kind of man and husband was the absent Lord Blackstone? Was he a villain and a rake? Or was he simply an ordinary man obviously bored with his wife's fragility?

I couldn't help but feel a bit betrayed by the Taylors. They had kept the odd situation at Blackstone Castle from me. Lenore Blackstone was not just a recovering young woman in need of a companion. She was a frail creature of delicate health, whether imagined or real, and there was more to her than a companion could cure. I could feel it. And the source of Lady Blackstone's ill health made me even more curious. I would find out what ailed Lenore Blackstone. I felt an instant connection with the beautiful woman who seemingly had chosen to spend her youth smothered among the pillows in her bed. And I knew Lenore had responded in kind. But still I wondered why Augustus Taylor had not been more forthcoming as to the true state of the Blackstones. And did Lord Blackstone have anything to do with his wife's condition? Did he even care?

I reached my room and quickly made ready for bed. I was exhausted and yet felt as I'd done nothing. I was happy to finally have a quiet time for myself. A shiver went through me as I eyed the room surroundings. The huge bed, with the heavy, deep red velvet draping welcomed, but the sheer size of the room instilled a sense of emptiness within me. What would life consist of here at Blackstone Castle? I was to keep a woman company whose husband obviously neglected her and whose personal maid seemed totally in control. And why did I feel Lenore was quite content to not be part of the Lord's attentions?

I had donned my sleeping gown and noticed how cold the room was. The fireplace was burning low but it should have been enough to keep me warm. Trying to keep my irrational fears under control, I peered around the room, my ears straining to catch any sound that didn't belong. Who had a key to my room other than Mrs. Patterson? Did Miss Drake have access to those keys?

I nearly jumped to the ceiling when a sudden rush of wind moaned through the chimney, blowing tiny embers in the fireplace. I reproached myself for acting like a foolish schoolgirl. Why had this castle caused such nervous fancies to take control of my thoughts? It could only be fatigue. Yes, I was incredibly fatigued and needed blessed rest.

I finally crawled into the cold bed, pulled the heavy bedcovers up over my ears and before long, drifted to a deep sleep.

Six

I awoke to a bright morning. I'd forgotten to close the heavy red drapes in my room the night before and the sun streaming into my room was beaming everywhere. I just had to fling open the windows, peer out at the glorious morning and take a deep breath. The trees below seemed to glow a deeper green. I inhaled deeply. The air here was crisp and clean and light, unlike the city. At my door, came a tap.

"Betsy, Miss." She opened the door and I couldn't help but smile as I noticed the pitcher of hot water in her hand. As she poured into the wash basin, she turned to me. "I'm to tell you that breakfast will be served in the breakfast parlor. Just ring for me and I'll show you the way, Miss."

My stomach was suddenly growling and hungry. I lost no time in dressing and found myself following Betsy, who as usual, showed up promptly once I called her. I made note to myself to make haste in learning my way around Blackstone Castle or I would quickly get lost. I preferred not to get confused in the huge castle. I knew not what dangers might trap me in some unknown part of the Blackstone Castle. I shuddered at the unsavory thought.

It was probably presumptuous of me, but I expected Lenore to join me for breakfast. But no, I ate my breakfast completely alone in a room that seemed to have never left the 17th Century. Large, heavy tapestries hung from the stone walls, with chandeliers and two large hearths at each end of the long, rectangular room. The table was nearly as long as the room and totally bare but for my sparse breakfast of eggs, marmalade and toast and thick sausages.

I was hungrier than I thought. I devoured a good portion of it, wiping my mouth delicately after the last of the toast. I was excited to find out what my first full day of being companion to Lady Blackstone would bring. I had no idea if Lenore was even awake at this early hour and since no one had come looking for me, I assumed she was still asleep or perhaps taking her breakfast in her own rooms.

Since I had time to spare and did not feel like spending that time back in my room, I thought it a most opportune time for a walk around the grounds. I had been intrigued by the aggressive and wide river that ran far below the cliff where Blackstone Castle towered, so I worked my way toward the west side of the castle, toward the edge of the cliff.

Bathed in the early morning sunshine, the castle no longer looked grim or somber as it had upon my arrival. It was such an exceptionally lovely morning, that I lifted my chin, closed my eyes for a moment and inhaled of the fresh air and warm rays. I decided to linger longer and stroll through the large gardens. They seemed to span the length of the castle. The layout was breathtaking at first view. I couldn't help but admire the work that went into growing and keeping such gardens. Beyond the gardens, to the east, thick woods beckoned. There was so much to the Blackstone grounds than merely the massive castle. I noticed a wide walk path leading into the woods and promised myself that I would explore the woods and the rest of the estate soon, hopefully, with Lenore at my side. I remain convinced more activity and long walks in fresh air would go a long way in ridding her of her malaise.

As I neared the edge of the cliff, I could hear the steady current of the wide, dark river that ran in a mad rush below. On the other side of the river, more thick woods crowded together. Large and roughly hewn rocks lay scattered along the river bank. It would mean certain death should anyone plunge from the cliff edge below. I was overcome with a cold dread and decided I should retreat and begin my walk back to the castle. I had to check in with Lenore before it got much later in the morning.

Making my way up the giant staircase and straight toward Lenore's room, I smiled as I felt the warm glow flow through me in anticipation of seeing her again. This was a new experience. One I very much wanted to indulge. Certainly, desiring the company of your employer was admirable, was it not?

I knocked lightly upon her door, the butterflies in my stomach running wild.

"Lady Blackstone, it's Miss Stewart."

I opened the door slowly. There was no one in the sitting room, but from the adjoining bedchamber, Lenore called out to me enthusiastically.

"Come in Miss Stewart."

She sat up in bed, drinking from a delicate tea cup while Miss Drake busied herself laying out the Lady's clothes. I did not want to proceed. The presence of the personal maid stopped me in my tracks. I stood a few feet from the door.

"Lady Blackstone," I said, keeping a gay tone to my voice, "I thought this a perfect morning for a walk."

"The sun is quite harsh for so delicate a complexion as your Ladyship's," Miss Drake said dryly, casting a stern look at Lenore.

Lenore sat, her mouth open, but said nothing.

"But I think you would enjoy being out in the sun and clean air. Even just across the gardens," I persisted. I wasn't going to allow Miss Drake to win. "I noticed a path down to the woods."

"Oh I would so love to walk with you, Miss Stewart, but I'm afraid we shan't be able to this morning for we must pay a morning visit to my mama-in-law. She will wish to see you right away."

A visit to meet the Dowager. I can't say it was the best substitute for a trek through the woods with Lenore, but my duties were clear. I was here to be companion to Lady Blackstone.

Miss Drake came forward silently, with Lenore's day shift and murmured deferentially. "If you're ready, my Lady..."

Lenore sighed and pushed back the layers of bed clothes. Did she mean to disrobe here, in front of me? Why did this cause such a blush within me? Why was I secretly smiling? And could I stop myself from staring? Not sure what I should do, I just looked away.

"Is there anything you wish me to do for you before we leave for the Dower House, Lady Blackstone," I managed to utter as I waited for her answer.

"Well, yes. I've been knitting the most perfect purse, but I think somehow, the pattern has gone terribly wrong. Do you think you can set it right for me? You shall find it in the large bureau in the sitting room."

I lingered longer than I should have, as I watched Miss Drake pull the night shirt over Lenore's shoulders. Lowering my eyes, I rushed out, nearly tripping, and went into the living room, found the purse atop the decorative bureau, found the nearest high back chair and began unraveling all the tangles Lenore had managed to create. It really took very little time, and I wondered at Lenore's lack of patience to fix the purse.

While working out the tangles, I managed to compose myself and waited patiently for the Lady Lenore. It seemed only minutes before she eventually emerged from her bedchamber dressed in a high waisted, dove gray dress which instead of adding color to her complexion, was far too colorless, in my opinion. Against the dullness of the gray, her fair hair appeared ashen instead of the glowing gold it truly was and her eyes paled and lost their brightness. Why had that miserable maid chosen such a horrid dress? And why wasn't Lenore more outspoken to her own needs and preferences?

The Lady Lenore Blackstone had the kind of extraordinary beauty that arrested anyone who looked upon her, and despite the drabby dress, I felt the tremble in my heart upon the sight of her.

With barely a look in my direction, Lenore sat down on the sofa facing the fireplace.

"Won't you please ring the bell, Miss Stewart, and let Gerald know that I should like the Barouche set round in half the hour. We shall be heading to the Dower House."

Lenore did not seem to wish to speak. It was hard to gauge her mood for I had not yet grown to know her and her inner self well, so I sat quietly fiddling with the purse on my lap once I pulled the bell rope.

Gerald, the footman, arrived promptly and I repeated what Lenore had requested. She remained withdrawn, staring at the cold hearth. What was ailing her? I excused myself quietly and swiftly went to my apartment to fetch my bonnet and light shawl. I was exasperated with Lenore. Why did she not make more of an effort to help herself? I had to find out what her physical condition really was. Was it in her head or was there something truly wrong within her? And why didn't she have a doctor attending her if that was the case? I was sure a walk to the Dower House would do the both of us better than a carriage ride. The house was not that far, for the chimneys were visible though the trees of the forest. But I had to be careful. I could not push Lenore too much. She was still very much an unknown quantity. I wanted very much to gain favor with the frail, beautiful Lenore.

I nearly ran back to the sitting room. Lenore had donned a dove gray silken pelisse with a white bonnet. Miss Drake hovered, extra wraps in her arms.

"Miss Stewart can carry these for you, my Lady, should you feel chilly on the journey."

She refused to address me and insisted instead on speaking as if I was not in the room. She handed me two shawls and a foot muff. This woman perplexed me. She came off as being utterly devoted to her mistress, yet I could not help thinking the solicitude fake. There was nothing I could do but keep my thoughts to myself and observe. Observe Miss Drake very closely.

Seven

I had to scramble to keep up with Lenore. She certainly was not lacking energy this morning. Was she that excited to see her mother-in-law or merely of the mind to get the visit over with quickly? Her mood had shifted as swift as lightning strike. Could I attribute it to the idea of getting away from the castle?

The carriage waited outside and I seated myself with my back to the horses, as befitted a mere companion. Lenore's mood brightened further as we bowled across the gardens and a blissful, tiny breeze fluttered the fringes of her parasol. She sat, her back stiff, seemingly enjoying the warm air and scenery. Beyond lay the large expanse of woods. As the carriage approached the looming trees, I noticed the lovely, colorful primroses sprouting profusely.

"Oh, Lady Blackstone, look at the primroses. Shall we come later to gather them?" I thought it the perfect invitation. The perfect plan to get Lenore alone, away from the prying, listening walls of Blackstone Castle. I had to begin to collect answers to my many questions. And not the least of reasons, I wanted so much to look into those fetching eyes and become lost in their depths.

She looked at me, her gaze curious, and smiled sweetly. "Yes, I think I should like that very much," she finally said, a wistful tone in her soft voice. She looked out the window, lost in thought. "I was married just a year ago, you know..." Pausing, she cast her look back upon me. "The village children scattered primroses as Foster and I left the church."

I watched her intently. I could not help myself. The porcelain look of her impeccable skin, the arch of light brown eyebrows, the thick lashes that fluttered with each movement of her eyes and the plump fullness of her lips kept me spellbound.

Lady Blackstone said nothing and I found myself at a loss for words. The silence was uncomfortable. My innermost belief was that she was not a happily married woman. Had it been an arranged marriage? Was Lord Blackstone an old, creased man or was he a handsome rake that women swooned over? I had so many questions that I yearned answers for.

Finally, I caught a glimpse of the towers of the Dower House.

"I think I can see the Dower House in the distance," I said, eager for some gaiety to the conversation. "Is it as old as Blackstone?" I asked.

"I can't really say," Lenore replied, leaning forward to look. "Victoria will know. She is Foster's younger sister and has a hand in running the estate. She is the expert in the history of Blackstone Castle and the surrounding land.

She knows it by heart and has entertained me for hours with her tales."

I remembered. *The woman on the racing horse with wild red hair flowing behind her.* "Oh, I think I saw Miss Blackstone on my journey here. She was at a full gallop riding opposite us."

"Yes, that would be Victoria," Lenore said, a big smile curling her lips. "She was here to call upon me and inquire after my health. She comes once a day when Foster is away."

The carriage rolled to stop in front of four columns and steps leading to wooden double doors.

"We've arrived," Lenore said abruptly.

The same groom that had brought me to Blackstone Castle helped the both of us from the carriage.

"James," Lady Blackstone said, "you may take the coach round back to the stable yard."

"Very well, my Lady." He bowed.

The Dower House was a newer construct than Blackstone Castle but nonetheless, an impressive piece of architecture. The four columns of stone jutted out from the front of the house, a circular balcony atop that led to the second floor. Part of the stone house was overgrown with climbing vines.

The butler who held the door open was expecting us and led us both into a sun-filled room that overlooked the lawns which framed the front of the house.

I stood in awe of the beautiful room and surroundings. But I'd barely had time to set my gaze on any one thing in particular when the double doors opened and the Dowager Blackstone walked in.

Lenore and the Dowager embraced lightly, barely touching.

"How are you, mama?" asked Lenore nervously. She turned to me briefly. "This is Miss Stewart."

I curtsied. "Pleased to meet you, Lady Blackstone." I took quick stock of the older lady before me. She was a slender, fashionably dressed woman who at first glance, had the appearance of younger years. But heavy powder and painted face could not conceal the wrinkles that caked in the creases. The Dowager had no doubt been a beauty in her day and apparently had no intention of surrendering to the ravages of time as long as cosmetics could help.

She eyed me with a quiet look.

"Go stand by the window so that I can see you in a better light," she ordered.

I wanted to stay put exactly where I was but did as she bid. I did not want to make things uncomfortable for Lenore.

After giving me a complete look-over, the Dowager uttered an audible "harrumph" and turned her critical gaze back to Lenore.

"Well, I daresay, I suppose Miss Stewart will do, but honestly, Lenore, you would have no need of a companion if you would simply pull yourself together. You sit about all day with nothing to do and that gives way to those low humours. You need to occupy yourself more usefully."

I found her treatment of Lenore unfair, but I could say nothing. Instead, cast my gaze to the floor. I hadn't liked the Dowager's tone on the word "companion."

"But there is nothing for me to do, Mama. I do not wish to interfere with Miss Drake and I know so little of anything useful." Lenore sounded so small.

"Why not strive to become more animated," continued the Dowager, "an independent woman can be desirable to the right man. You must force yourself to be lively. I daresay, Foster would not go away so frequently if he had a woman even half more conversational than you," declared the older woman. "Instead, he passes his time in town wasting his fortune in game clubs. If he continues like this, there will be little left of your marriage and the Blackstone fortune."

Tears dotted Lenore's lashes. I wanted to dry them away with my fingers and tell her she needed to be no one but herself.

"But...but...I don't know what to do. Foster is oblivious to anything I do or say and if I even reproach him, he rushes out of the room. How can I keep him there against his will?"

"Easy," the Dowager said vigorously. "Provide him with something to hold his interest..." she paused and cast a quick glance my way and then back to Lenore. "Find a way to give him an heir. It's been four months since your miscarriage. It was all very unfortunate, of course, but you must cease with your repining and work on the future. Once Foster holds his son to his chest, he will mend his ways. I'm certain. One doctor's opinion is not the final word."

"Yes," agreed Lenore meekly, bowing her head.

I stood quiet, trying hard to settle my blood from boiling during the rude exchange. If I could not speak up, then I preferred to slip out of the room to keep from interference and a quick end to my job. But I dared not walk out. I had learned to always stand up for myself and never allow anyone, no matter what class, to treat me as if I were not a proper human being. Being at the mercy of strangers taught me many things. Being witness to Lenore's humiliation was painful. I wished Lenore would stare down the Dowager and fight for herself. It was quite obvious that to the Dowager, a companion was no more than a piece of furniture. She had not acknowledged me since I walked into the room.

I glanced away and out the window and saw a rider coming along the path to the house. As the horse and rider got closer, I recognized it was the woman we had met the evening of my arrival at Blackstone Castle. Victoria Blackstone was working her way to Dowager House.

How many Blackstones must I be forced to meet in one day?

Eight

I did not wait long in anticipation. Victoria Blackstone entered the room, loose hair flowing down her shoulders. In the room of bright light and fingers of sun playing hide and seek with the retreating shadows in the corners, her hair appeared more like a deep, dark red, invoking the color of a glass of full-bodied Cabernet.

"Lenore, I saw your carriage in the stable. I knew you must be visiting. Are you better?"

The woman's voice was as deep as the color of her hair. She walked to Lenore and took both her arms, looking her over. The bright green eyes contrasted starkly with her dark hair.

Lenore became more animated and a blush bloomed on her cheeks. "Better, Victoria, thank you."

"Well, that is good news, of course." Victoria Blackstone removed her gloves and once she placed them on a delicate Mahogany table, glanced my way. And her gaze held me.

"Miss Stewart," the Dowager said, "this is my youngest daughter, Miss Victoria Blackstone. Victoria, this is Miss Stewart, who has come to be a companion to Lenore."

"It is my pleasure to meet your acquaintance, Miss Stewart," answered Victoria, a sly smile on her full, red lips. I became conscience of her long gaze and cast my own to Lenore. She finally looked back at Lenore.

"I do believe the spring air and sunshine has done you good, Lenore. Let's hope that now with Miss Stewart at your side, you will engage in daily walks."

The younger daughter of the Dowager was a tall and imposing woman. I had to admit that she captured my curiosity. She most certainly was a vision. The sight of her, basically dressed in men's breeches and boots, was startling and a bit alarming, but in a strangely attractive manner. Yet, I wondered, why did she not wear women's clothes? I had to put my imagination to rest for it had run wild with images of this stunning woman in a plunging neckline dress, hair piled high with jewels and a perfectly exposed neck. The very object of my fantasy was staring at me and that interrupted the crazy thoughts.

"Pardon me, Miss Stewart," she said, "I did not mean to startle you with my riding the other evening or with my...eccentric attire. I just detest the female clothes for riding. Mother indulges me although my brother condemns me. And then I cannot abide the side saddle business." She stopped and smiled. "It is easier to go about like this."

I had to admit, this Blackstone intrigued me. Would her brother equal that emotion? Or was he more like his mother? I hoped not.

A light conversation ensued, mostly not directed at me or involving a meager companion. All the while, Victoria Blackstone would look my way. At least she attempted to acknowledge me. Why did my stomach feel so tight and queasy? Why did her green gaze distress me so? Who was Lord Earl Blackstone's sister? And why did I want to know?

Abruptly, the Dowager asked for our carriage to be brought about. Evidently, the visit was over. Lenore kissed the Dowager and Victoria goodbye as the carriage pulled up. Miss Blackstone strode ahead and offered to escort us out.

She spoke softly to Lenore. "Do you have any news of when my brother is due to return?"

Lenore shook her head. "I never know, Victoria. He comes and goes at his own schedule, I'm afraid."

This caused a deep frown in Miss Blackstone's face. "I must see him when he does come about. Do send word, won't you?"

"There's nothing amiss, is there?" inquired Lenore.

Victoria patted her hand reassuringly. "No, no, my dear, nothing for you to worry over. It is merely some business we need to discuss." She flashed a smile and carried that smile over to me. "Once again, Miss Stewart, it has been a delight to meet you. I should hope we could see each other soon again at Blackstone Castle."

I looked away and smiled. I found very little to say. With that, both Lenore and I were sitting in the carriage and the horses picked up the pace. Lenore leaned back into the seat and sighed with relief.

"Thank God that is over and done with." She smiled at me, brighter than I'd seen her smile since I got to Blackstone. Without warning, she reached out and took my hand, her big, blue eyes sparkling. "I am truly thankful for you, Annalee. Now that the Dowager has approved of you, she will not be crusading for Foster to send you away which I feared she might do."

I had no desire to slip my hand from hers, proper or not. Lenore's touch was warm and it made me glow inside. The sound of my name upon her lips brought an odd, heady sensation. I became suddenly aware of the groom just above us and cast a warning glance in his direction. Lenore withdrew her hand and waved me off.

"Pay no heed to James. He is somewhat deaf so we can speak freely in front of him." Her gaze was steady on my face. "Were you not ready to leave the Dowager House? My mother-in-law makes me shake in my shoes. Can you not tell I am terrified of her?"

I agreed with her, of course, but the Dowager was simply an old woman who was accustomed to being treated like royalty. She needed someone to put her in her place.

"I shall be honest, Lenore, if I may. Her manner is more bully than mother-in-law."

Lenore sighed. "I cannot conceive how Victoria endures living with her. She is a handsome and kind woman and not lacking suitors, I am sure..." She lowered her voice. "I think I would marry the first decent prospect just to leave the unbearable Dowager." She laughed.

I could not control my outburst. "But knowing what marriage is like, would you truly recommend that to such a free spirit as Miss Blackstone?" I thought once again of the odd woman with male breeches and wild, wine-red hair and piercing green eyes. And then I remembered what Lenore had said of how disappointed she herself had been at the brutal reality of what marriage really was.

"Did you want to marry the Earl, Lenore? Did you love him?" I realized at once that my outburst and brazen questions could send me packing tonight, but it had been such a perfect time to ask those questions that had burned in my chest since arriving here.

I waited for her wrath or dismissal, but she did not answer me immediately. Instead, she stared out the window at the passing countryside.

"It would not have my choice," she said, quietly and hesitantly, still not looking at me. "It was something my own mama wished and Foster was so handsome and older and worldly. When he asked for my hand in marriage and mama swooned and went on and on, I thought it folly for me to refuse him..." She let the words drift off.

Did you love him, Lenore? I wanted that answer.

She turned back to me and her eyes were so radiantly blue that I thought I saw the sky reflected within them. They held me entranced.

"He is gone so often to town and the castle is so vast and gloomy that I have grown unhappy there. And then I lost the child..." She sighed deeply. "It was all for nothing."

I finally realized that I had some of the pieces of the puzzle that was Lady Blackstone already within my grasp. Her marriage was like so many; an arranged marriage to benefit parents. Lenore Marie LaSalle did not or ever love her husband, the Earl. I wondered why any woman, if once trapped into such a marriage, insist on continuing the charade? But then I nearly chuckled to myself. Of course women remained shackled to men they did not love in marriages that were mockeries. Who wanted to be a gypsy, traveling from rich employer to rich employer, the property of another human being? Choosing an inconvenient marriage might appear quite the attractive alternative. After all, what awaited unmarried women? What hope? Employment at some God-forsaken factory or servitude at a wealthy home, sharing the life of someone else's family as you watched like a shadow in the back room, or worse. The streets.

Lenore's sweet voice broke my melancholy thoughts.

"Annalee, now that you are here, it will be different." Her hand sought mine once again and this time, I could not mistake the shudder of excitement that coursed through me. But I could not allow this to continue. Not again. My desire for women had nearly caused a scandal for my father and I didn't need my own scandal at Blackstone Castle. Not now. Not here.

She was looking deep into my eyes. Too deep. "Annalee, I know I shall be in better spirits. Dear Annalee." She squeezed my hand gently. "And maybe that will bring good cheer to everyone at Blackstone." She smiled in a way that nearly caused me to visibly quiver where I sat.

I cleared my throat. "I think it extremely likely that you will feel better," I assured her. It was my job to encourage the Lady Blackstone to overcome her infirm condition. But, if I were successful, my work would be done and then where? Suddenly, I did not want to picture myself anywhere but with Lenore Blackstone.

And the inevitable idea came crashing into my thoughts. I did not want to meet Lord Blackstone. Better that he never return home. Of what use could he be to Lenore's rehabilitation? Without him in the way, I could devote all my time, everything, to her. But I was being foolish, of course. I knew he would come, and then I would be relegated to a few chosen moments with Lenore. After all, I was merely hired staff. A companion. But what if I could get Lenore healthy again? What if Lenore entertained thoughts of being Lenore Marie LaSalle again and not a burden to a bored and disappointed Earl?

And would she want me as a permanent...and meaningful companion?

Nine

I spent the previous night quietly in my room, plotting my plan. I felt certain I could get Lenore back to good health. The woman had no physical ailment. She suffered from neglect, lack of self worth and not enough healthy sunshine. Of that I was certain. She had lost her way in the darkness of this drafty castle. I would be her light. I would save her. Lenore Blackstone would have her knight in shining armor.

The following morning was a bright and fine day. I woke, ready to put my plan in motion. And it started well. I was able to convince Lenore to take a short walk in the gardens with me.

We walked, arm in arm, each with our own parasols, for the sky was brilliant but hot with the sun beaming down without mercy. I could not bear to not have her close. She was so thin, so frail. I wanted to wrap her up in my arms and protect her from the evils of the world. But she had a husband—an Earl, at that. For now, I satisfied myself in keeping her near me. Fascinated by the rapidly rushing river running below the cliff, I steered Lenore there.

"Have you ever gone below, to the river bank?" I asked her. Admittedly, the dark river had fascinated me. It appeared sullen and lonely, a dangerous place that existed so close to Blackstone Castle.

She paused and shielded her eyes as she looked at me. "No. I don't care for the river. Foster spends much time walking the river bank..." She paused, looked down. "I went once with him and the place darkened my spirits. He never asked me again."

Sensing that I had dampened her mood by inquiring about the river, I decided it best to head back to the castle instead. I squeezed her arm gently, smiling down at those shimmering blue eyes.

"Come now, Lenore, I think we've done very well today. We must do this each and every day."

Lenore and I had settled in the drawing room and the tea tray no sooner brought in, than a commotion outside in the great hall disturbed us. I was a bit startled by the booming male voice echoing beyond the door.

Suddenly, all the color drained from Lenore's face and her hand flew to her heart.

"Foster," she gasped. She cast a look of desperation at me. I confessed to being nervous at meeting the Earl of Blackstone for the first time. What did Lenore expect of me?

The door to the drawing room flew open and Foster Blackstone stopped in his tracks, a surprised look on his face. He was impressive and much taller than I imagined him. He stood surveying me with interest, wearing a rich burgundy coat with high collar, an ecru waistcoat, matching burgundy breeches and tan boots. His curly, dark hair was peppered with gray and his complexion vibrant. I was, however, uncomfortable in the way he stared at me. Why hadn't he even glanced at his wife?

"My dear Lenore, why was I not informed that we had such a lovely visitor at Blackstone?"

His teeth flashed in a wide smile as he approached us. Lenore got up immediately and I followed.

"But, Foster," fluttered Lenore, "she is not a guest...I mean, she is my companion. We did not expect you. How could I anticipate your return to Blackstone today?"

He stood before me, his gray eyes taking in every inch of me. Observing him closer, the Earl appeared to be far older than Lenore. Too old, yet still a handsome man, one I imagine any young woman would melt if offered a proposition of marriage. He finally cast his gaze to his wife.

"Well, my dear, I'm afraid it was all rather arranged in a hurry, you see," he admitted, "but I dare hope that my untimely arrival has not inconvenienced you and your new companion." He offered a slight bow to me. I opted to remain quite and only smiled.

"No, no, of course not," Lenore said hurriedly, "but I should inform Mrs. Patterson of your arrival."

He waved her away. "No need, my valet will have already done that."

"Have you had dinner?"

I noticed Lenore was trembling with nervousness. What was really going on in their relationship? Lenore Blackstone was afraid of this man.

His face grew impatient. "I've already dined at the Inn." He turned to me again. "Now, pray present me to your companion, my love."

"Of course, yes," Lenore said, distracted.

I was so desperate to reach out for her hand, to comfort her and let her know she was no longer alone. To talk her into standing up for her rights.

"This is Miss Stewart. You remember that she came recommended to your mama by Mr. Taylor."

"Ah, yes, I remember. Your servant, Miss Stewart," said the Earl with a grave face. "I trust you will find your life and duties here at Blackstone Castle to your liking."

"I am certain I shall, sir," I said, equally serious.

He finally turned his attentions back to his wife. I breathed a sigh of relief.

"And how is your health, my love? I hope there is some improvement." He eyed her closely. "I believe I see a trifle more color to your cheeks since I saw you last."

"I've been out on a walk today, round the gardens. I've been so sheltered that Miss Stewart thought daily walks could do me some good."

"Omniscient Miss Stewart."

His gaze shifted back to me. There was a cunning coldness in his eyes that reminded me of a wolf in hunting.

"I do believe, Miss Stewart," he continued casually, "that you may be quite right and gentle walks around the gardens and grounds will be most beneficial to Lady Blackstone."

"As her companion, I found it disturbing, when I arrived, for her to remain in her rooms all day and have told her so."

"I wholeheartedly agree," enjoined the Earl.

He never touched Lenore, but instead, he smiled and strolled to the door, his wife calling after him.

"We saw Victoria yesterday. She inquired as to your return back to Blackstone. I think she has business to discuss with you."

He stopped and turned around to look at Lenore. "I don't believe I shall trouble my sister tonight," he said blandly and offered a distracted smile. "I shall wait upon you later, my love. Good night, Miss Stewart."

"Good night, Lord Blackstone," I replied and then he was gone, the door closing behind him.

That was it? My introduction to Lord Foster Blackstone, the Earl, had been a short and perturbing one. The man did not love his wife and his wife most certainly did not love him. Of that I was without doubt. One thing I knew—his presence in the castle would put my plan for Lenore in serious jeopardy. Perhaps it was time for me to come down to cold reality. I was truly only a companion to Lenore Blackstone. There could be nothing more. Could there?

Ten

Lenore stared quietly at the closed door and then looked at me.

"Well," she said, "I was never as surprised as when Foster walked through the door. What brought him back to the castle, I wonder?"

"A desire to see you, I would guess," I blurted out.

"Do you think so?" inquired Lenore doubting.

Is he not your husband? Does he not live in his Castle?

"Of course, it may be so," I stammered. What could I say? Was it in my place to question her thus? "I think the Dowager will be pleased," I added quickly. "Do you suppose I should send a groom down with a note informing her and Miss Blackstone of Lord Blackstone's return?"

Lenore pondered the question for a moment. "There could be no harm in it, I think."

"Then I shall be happy to do it."

I scribbled a quick note and instructed Thomas to hand it to one of the grooms who was to ride out to the Dower House and deliver it post haste.

I waited for Thomas to leave the room and rose. "Perhaps it's best I say good night, Lenore." It wasn't what I wanted, of course, but the Earl was back and a companion would not be welcome in the Lady Blackstone's apartments.

But the alarm in Lenore's face was clear. "But you are not retiring to your room yet?"

"My Lady, if Lord Blackstone should return, he would not be pleased to find his wife's companion here," I reminded her gently.

She wanted me to stay. She wants me with her.

Lenore looked so forlorn that she was tearing my heart asunder. I was near ready to forget that her husband, the Lord of the Castle, my true employer, would claim his wife tonight. I would willingly stand up and face him, commanding Lenore stay with me. But no, as I looked at her with longing in my chest, I knew it was a mere fantasy. Sheer folly. If I whisked an Earl's wife away, I would never work in service again. What kind of life would be left to me then? Begging or prostitution in the streets was the bitter future. I left her with a curtsey and never looked back.

I laid awake nearly the entire night, refusing the call of the Sandman.

In the morning, I awoke with barely a peek of dawn drifting through my window. I was still dressed and felt sore throughout. Evidently, I had fallen into sleep at a very late hour. I knew I had not slept long, for every muscle in my body ached and was sore. My eyes refused to stay open.

Still, I washed my face and splashed my eyes, forcing them to do my bidding. I had barely changed my dress when word came from Miss Drake saying that Lenore would lie late abed and would summon me when ready. I pushed away the thoughts of her night in the arms of her husband.

Having changed and fully awake, I thought I would feed my increasingly hungry stomach. I decided to have breakfast and then go out for an early morning walk. I did not relish staying within the barren walls of the dreary castle on such a fine morning.

I ate breakfast alone, rather missing my frail Lady Blackstone sitting across from me. It was a bright day with a strong breeze stirring the leaves. The river below Blackstone Castle had fascinated me, and I thought to go down to the river bank and have a look around. Did the river have a name, I wondered.

I found the narrow dirt trail that led from the castle grounds down below and careful of the rather steep angle bordered by tall grass on both sides, I finally reached the river's bank. The water rippled past me. To the right, it stretched far out and to my left; it rounded the cliff and disappeared beyond. There was a structure of some sort that appeared like a tower, standing near the bank. On the far side, the tall trees grew close together, creating a wall of green darkness. I could imagine no one going into that dense forest. Casting my gaze above, I could only see the highest turrets of the castle reaching up into the blue sky.

The tower to the left beckoned to my curiosity. Intrigued by the mystery structure and being the brave woman I had trained myself to be, I walked toward it. I loved exploring. My father was fond of caves and I shall never forget the times we explored small caves during the picnics mountainside.

As I neared the tower, I discovered at its base a narrow, scarred oak door. I tried the long metal handle but it was locked. Whatever could such a structure be? What purpose could it serve? It was obviously not a lighthouse. What then?

Disappointed, I circled around the other side of it and was suddenly startled by the sound of hoofs. In the distance, from where I had come, there was someone approaching on horseback. For a fleeting second, my heart raced, daring to fantasize it could be—might be, Lenore. But did Lenore even know how to ride a horse?

But no, as the horse and rider neared, I saw that it was Victoria Blackstone. She was wearing a white lace collar shirt, male styled coat and breeches and black boots. How did she get away with wearing such clothing for a lady without scandal?

She reined in, dismounted and bowed. "Good Morning, Miss Stewart. You are abroad early."

"Good Morning, Miss Blackstone," I said, catching myself. "Or should I address you as Lady Blackstone?"

She smiled slightly and for the first time, I noticed the deep dimples that creased her cheeks.

"Not if you wish us to be friends."

It was an unexpected response. One I found I could not answer.

"It was such a bright morning," I continued, trying to cover my lack of comeback. "I could not resist exploring the river bank. Does it have a name? The river, I mean?"

"Blackheart," she said, looking out at the quickly moving water. "They say the bottom of the river, the sediment, is as black as night. That is why the water is so dark."

The way she looked at me caused my stomach to jump nervously...but in a giddy kind of way. I cast my gaze to the tower.

"I was going to try and explore that old tower, but the door is closed, so I could not go inside."

Victoria Blackstone shook her wild mane of red. "I would not advise that, Miss Stewart. It is unsafe to do so. The stone work is crumbling." She moved past me, reaching a hand to several stones that had fallen off completely. "See here, the stones are coming loose."

I watched her. After finally meeting her brother, the Earl, I could actually trace a family likeness between them, but the Earl was darker, while Victoria's features were softer and her complexion fair.

She was once again staring at me in a most disarming way. I felt compelled to break the silence.

"You will be aware that Lord Blackstone returned yesterday."

She nodded. "Yes, we received the message and I was actually on my way to see my brother but wanted to take a ride by the river. I guess we had the same thought..." She paused and looked out toward the river. "This place retains a sense of the raw and primordial. It soothes my soul."

She moved closer to me. The breeze I had enjoyed earlier had become a stronger wind, sending the tall trees across the river swaying and dancing, the leaves rippling. Victoria Blackstone was an enigma to me. She wore men's clothing and held more power in the running of

Blackstone than most women were ever allowed. And why did she stare at me thus?

"I must not detain you, then, Miss Blackstone." I wanted to walk away but she reached out and took hold of my arm.

"Please, Miss Stewart, if I may speak to you about Lenore, Lady Blackstone." She eyed me with softness in her eyes. "I know you came to her as a companion, but Lenore needs a friend. I have tried but I fear she connects me too closely with my brother and cannot fully trust me. I hope—I trust, Miss Stewart, that you can sustain both roles."

I was somewhat surprised and shocked at the unexpected request and also by the touch of her hand; the familiarity that is not shared between a Lady of her class and those in service.

I cleared my throat and met her pleading gaze. "I shall do my best, of course. I believe that if I can persuade Lady Blackstone to widen her interests and physical activities, it must improve her spirits."

Victoria Blackstone's face beamed. "Those are excellent ideas and you may rely on my total cooperation. I care for Lenore a great deal and am always at the ready to help her stand up to my brother. He can be a formidable bully."

The wind blew through her hair and swept it across her face. The quiet moment between us grew too long. She smiled finally and bowed quickly.

"Good day, Miss Stewart. I'd best attend to Foster."

She mounted and rode away, leaving me alone and suddenly consumed with a chill from the wind that had grown too cold.

Eleven

As soon as I reached the castle, cursing myself for dragging mud from the river on my shoes, I brushed it off as quickly and best as I could and went at once to Lenore's apartment.

Would he be there?

I pushed the thought from my head. My fears were unfounded. Lenore was wearing a morning gown of the palest pink and unfortunately, Miss Drake stood brushing her hair. They both looked at me as I entered the room.

I wanted to grab Lenore's hands, kiss them and stare into her eyes, but settled for mundane conversation.

"Good Morning, Lady Blackstone, Miss Drake. I've been down to the river bank this morning," I said, not bothering at all to even look at Miss Drake. "The breeze was delightful until the wind got too frisky."

Lenore sighed, her gaze lingered on me. "I wish I could feel equal to walking this morning. As it happens, I have mislaid my shawl. Have you perchance seen it, Miss Stewart?"

"You may have just laid it down somewhere," I offered, wishing Miss Drake would stop doting on Lenore and leave. "Suppose I go downstairs and look for it?" The truth was, I did not wish to be in the same room with Miss Drake. I did not trust her.

Excusing myself, I nearly ran down the wide stairs and upon reaching the bottom, saw the Earl coming out of the library in a rush.

"Some other day, my dear sister. There can be no urgency over the matter," he was saying over his shoulder. Was Victoria in the library?

I came to a stop and he spotted me.

"Oh, Miss Stewart," he said, a wide smile forming. "Good Morning."

He wore a deep blue coat with fawn buckskin pantaloons and polished boots. The Earl took a step toward me, but just as he did so, Victoria Blackstone emerged from the library, her face set in anger. She did not even pay me attention.

"But this is urgent," she insisted. "The roof of the stable needs immediate repair. The rain is leaking in at several places"

"Well then, it most certainly must be attended to," replied the Earl, feigning interest. "Bring it to my notice again or have mother bring someone in from the village."

With not another word or glance, he was out the door. Victoria stood staring after him, fists clenched at her side. Completely ignoring me, she left after the Earl without a word.

It troubled me to have come into the confrontation. I told myself it was no concern of mine. Brothers and sisters were prone to quarrel. So I put the whole scene from my mind and went in search of Lenore's shawl. I began my search in the hall. And found it. It had slipped behind a chest at the center of the hall.

I immediately took it back to Lenore. Miss Drake was still in the room, arranging Lenore's dress for the day. In Lenore's eyes I could see her desire for me to stay but I could not.

I went back to my rooms and had barely changed into my only other decent day dress, when Betsy knocked on my door with an apologetic curtsey.

I laughed as I buttoned the last clasp. "Oh, don't be silly, Betsy. Stop all that curtseying and treating me like royalty. I'm a servant. Staff, like you."

She eyed the floor. "Yes, Miss. I'm to inform you that luncheon is served in the Dining Room, Miss." She nearly curtsied again, but smiled sheepishly and rushed out.

Now that the Earl was back, luncheons were being served in the Great Dining Room. I did not look forward to it.

Thankfully, the dinner was uninspired and passed quickly. The Earl seemed pre-occupied, hardly glancing at Lenore but polite to me, attempting mundane conversation such as asking after my life at Mrs. Bentley's. I could not help but see that there was much unhappiness lurking at Blackstone Castle. But there was also something with a darker undertone. Something I could not yet put my finger on. It whispered from the walls, from the river below, from the shadows.

Lenore refused most of the dishes. I cast swift glances toward her, but she kept her eyes downcast, attempting to move the food around her plate. Never at a loss for an appetite, I appreciated all the food. I had not eaten like this since Father and I were still part of the upper social circle with a big house and staff. Grateful for being allowed to sit at the table with the Lord and Lady Blackstone, I had no qualms eating everything brought to me. But I could not say that I was sorry when Lord Blackstone finally rose from the table.

He bowed and excused himself, saying he had business to attend in the village and that he would be back before nightfall. Left alone with Lenore, I moved closer to her side, searching her face.

"You hardly touched your food. Are you feeling ill?"

She smiled that sweet smile that made her look like a little girl instead of a grown, beautiful woman.

"I am glad he is gone." She reached for my hand, but one of the servants entered the room, followed by another, and they began removing the leftover food and cups and plates. Lenore grabbed my hand nonetheless and pulled me away, out the door. "Let's go to the sitting room," she said.

Did she realize that I would follow her anywhere? But just as we reached the main hall, the door bell rang out. Lenore and I froze in mid step. The butler who had let me in when I arrived appeared and opened the door.

The Dowager strolled in, removing her gloves and ignoring the butler. She spotted us immediately. With not a sign of a smile or greeting, she came to stand before us. She barely glanced at me and focused her intense gaze on Lenore.

"This is very unpleasant, having to come looking for my son. I cannot conceive why Foster has not paid his respects to his own mother," she grumbled. "It's the duty of a son to do so..." She paused and squared her shoulders. "You should have reminded him, Lenore."

"But I thought he had visited you at the Dower House this morning," said Lenore, placating the old woman.

"Well, you assume wrong. He did no such thing. I assure you, he will hear about this." She looked up at the stairs. "Where is he? I wish to speak to him."

"He just left, Mama."

"Good Heavens! Again?"

"He assured me he would return tonight."

The Dowager was clearly not happy. She shook her head.

"I suppose I did not waste my trip since you are here. I have news that you must pass on to Foster. A very dear and trusted friend of mine, Sir William Birnbaum, has leased Dorset Manor and will reside there for the duration of the season, perhaps longer. He will be an asset to the neighborhood. There is, shall I say, a great deal of money that Sir Birnbaum brings with him, all made from the sugar plantations in the West Indies. And his only son is sole inheritor. I've not seen the boy since he was a tot. Sir Birnbaum now wishes him to take his place in society, marry and bring up a family. He has solicited my help in suggesting his son to eligible ladies."

I thought she would never finish. I wanted her to leave. To leave before the day was gone and my time with Lenore vanish as well. But I realized Lenore could not just rush her Mother-in-Law out the door.

"It will be very agreeable to have an addition to our local society circle," Lenore said, neither excited nor bored. "How old is the younger Mr. Birnbaum?"

"Not above five and twenty, I should imagine. It was unfortunate that he lost his mother at birth. Sir Birnbaum has been a good father, but he wants his son established in the family business and well married before he is too old to enjoy grandchildren. I doubt he would have trouble, I assured him. John Birnbaum would be the most eligible of bachelors..." She paused and frowned. "If only Victoria were more open to suggestions. But I have not given up all hope with that child. When she sees him, she may be immediately smitten."

I pictured the wild tresses flying in the wind and the male attitude—and the way Victoria Blackstone looked at me—and would have given anything to be able to have told the Dowager that her daughter would not be easily smitten by a man nor be willing to be tamed into marrying. But I could not utter a word, of course.

She continued, barely taking a breath. "And this is why, my dear, I intend to give a dinner party on the last Friday of this month. It is my way of introducing John Birnbaum to Victoria. You and Foster are free on that date, I trust, Lenore?"

"I am certain we shall be."

Lenore had no choice but to be able to attend. Would I go? Would Lenore want me by her side even if the Lord Blackstone was there? Wishful thinking could be so disastrous to the soul.

"Good," the Dowager said. "Remember not to engage yourself to anyone else." She abruptly turned to me, as if she noticed a particular object in the room. "I shall require your help, Miss Stewart. You will need to send out the invitations for me and write out the place cards for the table. I have no one I can spare at the Dower House."

I nodded, surprised. "Certainly, Lady Blackstone."

Satisfied, she placed a quick kiss on Lenore's cheek, donned her gloves and was out the door without another word to me or Lenore.

Lenore looked at me and let out a breath as she shook her head.

"Poor Victoria. Her mother has found another eligible bachelor for her." Her lips curled into a mischievous smile. "She won't like this one any better than the others. But the Dowager will not rest until her daughter is married off. She just won't realize that Victoria has a mind of her own and isn't a child."

Lenore took my hand again, excitement in her sparkling blue eyes.

"What shall I wear to the dinner party? I have not been out and about in society for so many months that I will have to get something new and pretty."

Whatever private moment might have been afforded us disappeared in a puff of the promise of a glittering dinner party. Thoughts of new dresses and what to wear completely took over Lenore's focus. She ran up the stairs in search of Miss Drake so that they could search her closets or arrange for a new dress to be made. I was left once again, alone and wondering what my job really was at Blackstone Castle.

It turned out that Lenore arranged for bales of shimmering silk to be sent from the finest seamstresses in Lustleigh to be inspected for a new dress. I remember the workmen bringing in bales of a rainbow of colored silk. I was mesmerized by the fabrics that took up every inch of Lenore's apartment.

I urged the merits of a royal blue which enhanced the color of Lenore's eyes, but instead, she settled upon a lilac, which while exquisite, did little to bring out the overpowering essence of Lady Blackstone and those hypnotizing blue eyes.

I saw little of Lenore after that, but busied myself with the drudgery work of addressing the dinner invitations to a party I was not good enough to rate an invitation to. A party that was like so many I had had the privilege of not only attending, but hosting in my early years.

No one promised me that my days would always be carefree and full of wealth, but neither did I even in my wildest dreams, imagine them like this.

Twelve

I was nearly bored to tears until the day of the dinner party. Lenore refused to allow me in her apartment, wanting to keep her dress a secret. She spent her days with Miss Drake, I imagined, as the dark woman fussed about and fitted her for the dress.

Lord Blackstone was equally scarce, having made an appearance through the hallway only to exit the castle daily. What could keep him away from his ravishing wife and duties at Blackstone? Whenever Victoria desired her brother's attention and aid for whatever the reason, she was obviously pushed aside. Was everyone dinner party crazy?

The grand dinner party day finally arrived and I fully expected to spend my day and evening alone, but a groom from the Dower House arrived late morning with a message from the Dowager. Evidently, I had become her own personal servant, for I was to spend the afternoon at the Dower House helping to arrange the flowers. I suppose I should have been grateful for the varied duties my position afforded me. Certainly, I was spending less and less time with Lenore. Would I be sent away? No, I could not leave her side. I would do anything to stay at Blackstone Castle.

When I arrived at the Dower House, I found that the hot houses had been nearly stripped of all the choicest blooms. I was given instructions by one of the maids and was nearly done adding the finishing touches to a fern trailing from the silver epergne in the center of the large table in the sitting room, when the Dowager herself rushed into the room, face creased into a disturbed look, lips pursed.

"Could there ever be a more unfortunate time to fall ill! Now the dinner guest seating will be completely upset unless I can find someone to take old Mrs. Wallis's place..." She paused. "How am I to do that in such late notice? There is no help for it."

Whoever was she speaking to, I wondered. As usual, she completely ignored my presence in the room.

But suddenly, she looked directly at me. "You. You will make up the number, Miss Stewart."

"I, Lady Blackstone?" To say I was surprised would have been a monumental understatement.

"Yes, girl, you. Now, stop what you are doing and go back to the castle and tell Lenore that you are to be part of the party tonight. The note from the Dean's wife just arrived. She has contracted a feverish chill and is confined to her bed. I should be beside myself if both she and the Dean do not come, so both he and you must be here tonight."

Excited, I quickly grabbed my bonnet from the table after excusing myself and opted to walk back to Blackstone Castle. Truth was, I ran through the woods, grappling with the new problem the dinner party posed. A formal dinner party held no terror for me. I had acted as hostess for my father on many such occasions. But in those glory days, I had a large and rich wardrobe at my disposal. But all my beautiful dresses and jewelry had long been sold. We had to pay off gambling debts. I had nothing left that could be construed as formal wear. There was no helping me. I would have to swallow what little pride I had left and appear in the same grey dress I wore for dinner at the castle each night. Heavens, it looked shabby enough there, at the Dowager's dinner party, it would present an appalling contrast. It was true that a companion was expected to be drabby beside her Lady, but I could not help remember all my lovely dresses with longing, including my favorite—a primrose satin scalloped with blonde lace and a white lute string spangled with silver. My heart felt the bitter pang. All of it had been swept away.

I went directly up to Lenore's room, my heart beating like the wings of a soaring bird. I didn't care if Miss Drake was there or not. I would be going and she was not. It gave me a certain sense of delight.

I found Lenore quite alone, resting with her head back on her mountains of pillows. I was afraid I'd frightened her with my hasty entrance. But she smiled wide, her blue eyes alive.

"Oh, Annalee, have you finished the flowers? I thought the Dowager would keep you all day."

"No, Lenore. It is wonderful news," I said, not caring to hide the excitement in my voice. "There has been a change of plans. The Dean's wife has taken ill and I am to take her place tonight to make even guests at the table!"

At first, Lenore's mouth opened as she sat up straight, but then a look of concern took hold.

"But whatever shall you wear, Annalee? That is, perhaps you have a gown which I have not seen yet?"

All the shame came rushing back and my whole body sagged under the weight of regret.

"No," I answered quietly. "I shall be obliged to wear my gray dress, but it will not signify, for no one will notice me."

Lenore rose quickly from her seat and came to stand close to me, her hand resting on my arm. I inhaled the smell of her and it made me quiver. She searched my face.

"If only we had known of this sooner, my dear Annalee."

The way she said my name made me nearly melt from within. But I had to remain in control. Lenore's eyebrows wrinkled in thought.

"I would gladly offer any of my dresses but you are so much taller than I that they would be too short for you and beyond help. I cannot think of any that could be let down."

Then suddenly, her face brightened. "But wait, there is a dress, a white gauze which was far too long and never altered for me. It would be perfect for you! Even if it might be a bit short, the length could be fixed without a doubt, I think!"

She smiled wider. "Ring for Miss Drake. She is very fast and there is time for her to do it if she hurries."

Oh no, I thought. That woman would rather quit her position than help me.

"Are you sure, Lenore? It would not be an imposition on your Miss Drake?"

Before my words faded in the room, Lenore had rushed to the pull cord and summoned Miss Drake. I was not sure I wanted the dour, gray woman involved in anything to do with me, but I could not refuse my invitation, however obtained, to a brilliant dinner party at the Dower House. And besides, Lenore wanted me there. That had to mean something.

As I suspected, Miss Drake showed up with the usual suspicious glances directed at me. She was reluctant to even search for the dress, let alone work on the alteration to fit me.

"The Dowager has requested Miss Stewart's presence for the dinner party tonight, Miss Drake, so I'll have you please fetch the dress you personally put away. It will be a tad short I suspect, for Miss Stewart, but since she has nothing ready to wear of her own, we shall add a band of lace to the hem. We need it tonight, Miss Drake, so please work in haste."

I was so proud of my Lenore. She'd been firm with the stern woman. She'd left Miss Drake with no recourse for objection. The will of the Dowager was not to be ignored, after all. I wanted to chuckle out loud.

Miss Drake cast a quick glance at me, nodded and left the room. I didn't think she left happy. If I could, I would have kissed Lenore right then and there for her brave stance with the unlikable woman. We both decided it would be best that I wait in my own room for Miss Drake. The alterations would not take long.

I did not want to leave Lenore. We had spent such little time together since Lord Blackstone returned home. I continued to fear that my service as companion was becoming less required. Was he planning on going away again and leaving Lenore alone?

A firm knock came upon my door. Miss Drake held the dress cradled in her arms and a small bag under one arm. She went directly to my bed and spread the dress out evenly and gently. My eyes took in every detail of the dress. I could not help but reach out and run my hand across it, hesitantly, for I feared Miss Drake might rebuke me for touching it.

It was the softest French gauze, its filmy white was scattered all over with tiny stars. So enraptured was I by the sheer beauty of the dress, that I did not notice the cold stare of the woman in the room with me. Her mere presence could drain any cheer from me. For now, however, I was beholden to her for the help. She was my ticket to look the lady I knew I was at the party.

"Please excuse me," I said. I began to remove my dress.

Without a word or emotion, Miss Drake helped me pull the exquisite gown over my head. To my amazement, the dress fit as if made for me, short of a few inches at the bottom.

Miss Drake pulled a long roll of lovely and delicate lace from her bag and quickly began to pin it to the bottom. I decided to deal with my extreme discomfort by not moving or even looking down at what she was doing. I just stared ahead as still as a statue, letting my mind imagine the glittering event of the dinner party.

It seemed like I stood that way for hours but I was certain it must not have been that long. Miss Drake, finally done, stood up and gave me a sullen look.

"I will need to finish the alterations and return the dress to you as quickly as I can."

I removed it, being extra careful, and laid it over her arms. Then she was gone. I let out a big breath of relief and lay back upon the bed. Why did that woman have such an ill effect on me? The whole ordeal had left me drained. I felt my eyes grow heavy and thought I could take an afternoon rest before Miss Drake returned the dress.

I must have dozed off for I was awakened by a strong and persistent knock on my door. How long had I slept?

It was Miss Drake, with dress in hand and a pair of white satin sandals and gloves.

"The Lady Blackstone advises you wear these sandals with the gown this evening. She hopes they fit."

She handed me the gown, sandals and gloves and walked briskly away. I watched her as she disappeared into the shadows of the hallway and closed the door, hardly able to control my excitement.

I washed up, donned new undergarments and slipped the dress on, being careful with each pull of the fabric. I stood surveying my flushed cheeks in the mirror before me. I thought I resembled Cinderella going to the big ball. For this evening, I could imagine myself back in the past when a dinner party was a common occurrence and my Father's proud glance told me that I'd done him credit.

Well, tonight I would make the most of this brief excursion into society and make Lenore proud. I would try not to remember that tomorrow I would be no more than a companion once again.

To my ingenuity, I had succeeded in keeping at least one glorious piece of my past, a velvet cloak. Though now rubbed in places, it would serve beautifully to drape over my dress.

I'd barely finished putting the finishing touches to my hair, when Betsy came to my room to say the Lord and Lady Blackstone waited downstairs with the carriage. Never one to do very well with my own hair, I thought it looked presentable enough.

As I made my way down the huge stairs, I saw Lenore. The sight of her took my breath away. He lilac dress was accented with matching gloves and a white cape with a collar that rose up behind her head. Her hair was piled high, thick and lustrous, confined by a satin riband. Enchanting rings of golden hair fell on her brow. And I'd been wrong. The lilac of the gown made her blue eyes glow.

So spellbound was I with Lenore that I barely noticed the Earl. He stood quietly smiling and wore a velvet coat and breeches of the blue so deep that it almost appeared purple. White socks and blue shoes completed his dinner dress.

"My Lady and her companion look amazingly vibrant and lovely this evening." His eyes held mine but I looked away. He extended his arm toward the door. "The coach awaits us as does my very impatient mother."

As the coach pulled away from the castle, I could not keep my gaze from Lenore. My heart was beating so hard that I was afraid I might faint from the sheer thrill running through me.

If only I could have her only to myself tonight. If only.

Thirteen

I was thankful the Earl was particularly quiet on the ride to the Dower House, content to watch the scenery go by. Lenore appeared somewhat jittery, uncomfortable. She cast quick glances my way, a slight smile set upon her lips. I tried hard not to stare and not to inhale too deeply of the scent she wore. It was divine.

There were several carriages at the door of the Dower House, but Lord Blackstone was the main attraction. Once we arrived, it was as if the Black Sea had parted. Lenore and I divested ourselves of our cloaks and were immediately ushered into the salon.

The Dowager took both the Earl and Lenore away with barely a nod to me. As usual. I was at least pleasantly surprised that she cast her gaze up and down the length of me. Did she recognize Lenore's dress? No, Lenore had never worn it. Had the Dowager approved of my gown?

I watched, standing alone and feeling out of place and a total stranger, as the Dowager led Lenore and Lord Blackstone to the guest of Honor, Sir William Birnbaum. I assumed that the young man standing beside Sir Birnbaum was his son, John Birnbaum.

I made haste to find the coziest corner of the room, a place I could study the eligible bachelor Mr. Birnbaum. He was certainly what most women would consider handsome. His raven curls fell slightly on his forehead and his dark brown eyes contrasted a fair skin and a firm jaw. As he took Lenore's hand and placed a kiss, deep dimples formed on his cheeks. Any woman not Victoria Blackstone would indeed be smitten by John Birnbaum. But as he shook the Earl's hand firmly, I noticed that Victoria was nowhere in the vicinity. I had expected him to be dancing attendance on her, but it was not the case.

Searching the room thoroughly, I perceived her on the far side of the room talking to an imposing matron. And not only that, but I nearly gasped as I saw her. Victoria Blackstone was dressed as a proper lady! Was that really her? Yes, I was sure of it. That color of hair and the brilliant green eyes were unique. She wore a rich blue gown, accented with gold which seemed to sparkle in her hair, which was for once, piled in a delightfully stylish design atop her head and topped with a gold ringlet. If I didn't know any better, I would have believed this was a twin. It appeared to me that Miss Blackstone had found the furthest spot in the room to her mother and the Birnbaum men.

I stayed close to my corner and continued observing how expertly Miss Blackstone avoided getting caught by the Dowager. She flitted like a butterfly between guests, never stopping long enough to be spotted. I had to admire her and felt some pity for her plight.

But suddenly, the butler announced that dinner was served and I was certainly glad about that. I was famished. I found myself partnered with a young lady who was introduced as Clarisse Wallis, the Dean's daughter. Evidently, the Dean had elected to stay with his ailing wife and not wishing to insult nor ruin the Dowager's dinner, sent his daughter in his stead. She was quite a lovely woman, with almond-shaped blue eyes and a pleasing figure. She sat to my right and to her right, the Earl and Lenore.

To my left was a red-faced man whose sole interest seemed to be in horses. Fortunately, due to my father's evil obsession with horse racing, I at least was able to engage the man in semi-intelligent conversation. I could not say the same for the young Miss Wallis beside me. She seemed completely entranced by the Earl of Blackstone. She laughed at his every joke and leaned in far too close when they spoke. He seemed to be encouraging it. It made my skin crawl and I wished I could leave the room and take Lenore with me. Her husband was blatantly flirting with the Dean's daughter for all to see while his wife sat meekly beside him.

I was nearly bored to tears by the red-faced man's conversation and had gotten very good at feigning interest while keeping an eye on the growing friendliness of Miss Wallis and Lord Blackstone on my other side. I was relieved when finally the ladies all rose and en masse drifted to the drawing room. The men were left to their port. I could not locate Victoria, who I was happy had a respite from having to find escape from the young Mr. Birnbaum and her mother.

Lenore had gone and found herself a spot on one of the sofas but before I could find my way to join her, Miss Wallis seated herself and took away my space. I stood quietly to the side, offering a smile to Lenore. She smiled back but looked perturbed by Miss Wallis's presence.

"Dear Lady Blackstone," the woman cooed, "May I speak to you? I've never come to many of these dinner parties because my papa and mama always love to attend and always keep their invitations. But I am fortunate to be able to be here in my papa's place since he chose to with my mama—her fever and all..." She paused and looked at me, no doubt wondering who I was and what I meant by standing so close.

"Well," she continued, "I just wanted to say that I have heard so much about Lord Blackstone and Blackstone Castle. It must be such a remarkable place. I so long to see a real castle."

I wanted to gasp out loud. It was the most blatant of hints, but Lenore was not sophisticated enough to parry it. Lenore forced a smile.

"Well, I shall be happy to welcome you there," she stammered.

The sneaky and sly Miss Wallis seized the opportunity. She smiled like a toothy hyena.

"Then I shall lose no time in paying you a visit. I so dote on ruins and have often attempted to convince papa to a trip to the ruins of Rome in Italy."

"Blackstone is certainly old, but it's not yet in ruins," Lenore began, but was interrupted when the gentlemen guests began to join us.

The Earl walked briskly across the room and stood leaning on the back of the sofa, his attention divided between Lenore and Miss Wallis. I was ignored.

"My love," he said to Lenore, "You appear quite serious. Has Miss Wallis been confiding her intimate secrets to you?"

More like she already confided them to you over dinner.

I felt my thoughts to be true. It wasn't hard to see now what kept the Lord Blackstone away from his home. But was this part of his nature or behavior acquired during the course of the obviously failed marriage?

Miss Wallis blushed attractively and on cue.

"Certainly not, Lord Blackstone, though I am persuaded they would be safe with your lovely wife. No, I was telling her how very much I love old architecture and how much I have wanted to visit a real castle. Your wife kindly invited me to visit Blackstone Castle and I intend to take her at her word." She paused and cast the Earl an unmistakably coy glance. "I warn you, I shall not rest until I have explored every inch it."

"That will take some time, Miss Wallis," said the Earl in a smooth voice. "But how could we be better occupied?"

Miss Wallis only looked at him thoughtfully. I was finding it more and more difficult to control myself. I moved ever further away, toward the corner, deciding to remain a distant spectator so as not to get myself in trouble with an outburst. If it wasn't so disrespectful to Lenore, I could find it amusing to try and guess what exactly the Earl thought of this lady?

I wanted to lean even further into the comfortable corner of choice when I suddenly became aware that someone was at my elbow, close behind me. I turned and was surprised to see Victoria Blackstone at my back.

Fourteen

"Good evening, Miss Stewart," she said, an amused look in her eyes. "It was most kind of you to oblige my mother on such short notice."

"Not at all, Miss Blackstone," I said, aware how truly remarkable this woman's green eyes were. "At the risk of sounding like an absolute selfish bore, I secured for myself a very pleasurable evening."

She cocked her head slightly. "You mean you enjoy being hidden away in a corner," she responded in mock surprise, eyebrows raised.

I had to laugh. "You have me at a disadvantage there, but indeed I am content to be a looker-on. Forgive me, Miss Blackstone, it is difficult to say this without sounding ungrateful, but you must know that a companion does not expect a gay life."

She shook her head slowly, still smiling. "No, I imagine she would not keep her position long if she did."

She paused, looked toward the growing crowd of ladies and gentlemen gathering. "You know, Miss Stewart, it strikes me that you have not yet seen the orangery. I should be happy to give you a personal tour."

Was she asking me to leave the dinner gathering with her? Surely, I could not refuse her. She was, after all, the Earl's sister. Besides, I'd had nearly enough of Miss Wallis.

"I should very much like to see it," I said, still surprised by the invitation, yet realizing it afforded Victoria Blackstone the perfect escape from her mother and the bachelor. That had to be the motive.

She suddenly grabbed my arm and escorted me quickly through some of the people until we were outside. The night air was brisk and there was a hint of a breeze. It was almost enough to wish I had my cloak. The orangery had windows on the south wall running from floor to ceiling and opposite to them, niches containing marble busts. Below each bust sat an orange tree in a tub. There was a woman and a man strolling along at a leisure pace, admiring the trees. They paid us no heed.

Victoria led me to the furthest niche, filled with shadows and the most removed from the windows and the view inside. We ducked under the larger orange tree and I leaned up against the wall as she stood opposite me. I didn't think anyone could see us. I began to wonder what this little excursion was really about.

"I trust you will not feel too chilly," she said, "but the evening is rather mild and I shall try not to keep you too long." She was staring at me again and I could not but admire her choice of color for her dress. The deep blue had turned nearly purple in the darkness of the night. And her eyes...

"Miss Stewart, you're smart enough to have gathered I brought you out here because I do have something particular to say to you...concerning Lenore, and I was afraid of being overhead or interrupted in the drawing room."

Definitely would have been heard and interrupted in the drawing room.

"I understand perfectly well," I said. "If there is some service you wish me to perform, please tell me. I want anything that will make Lady Blackstone a whole woman again."

If she only knew.

For once, the fiery woman before me seemed hesitant.

"I want you to do all you can to rouse her," she said at last. "Lenore has become prone to sinking into fits of melancholy and I wonder if the fits bring on the ill physical health or the complete opposite. She is a young woman and she should be enjoying life instead of shut away from others her own age."

Others like you?

The jealous thought came unbidden. But the interest of the Earl's sister for Lenore was perplexing to me. I, of course, had a plan for Lenore. But I wasn't going to share it with Victoria Blackstone. I had no notion who she really was. Was she truly a concerned friend or a spy for the Earl?

"Of course, I think you are quite right," I said, interested in hearing what more she had to say. "As I've said, I have managed to persuade her to walk a little in the park from time to time, but she seems to tire so easily. However, now that the Lord Blackstone is home again—"

"He will not help her!" She spoke so loudly that she turned to see if anyone had heard.

I could only stare at her in shocked surprise.

"I beg your pardon," she said with obvious effort. "My brother has his own occupations which Lenore cannot share..." She shook her head. "No, something is called for which would engage her interests, get her out and about."

And it suddenly occurred to me.

"A puppy," I said. "A small breed of dog. I recollect her saying once that she thought she might like to have a spaniel, and since it would have to be exercised, it would take her out into the air and give her something to think about apart from her ills."

Victoria's face broke into a most charming smile. "That's a capital idea." She suddenly inched closer to me and I moved back against the wall. The bricks were cold on my back. I didn't quite know why, but I felt I had to keep the conversation going. Her gaze had grown intent and the sparkle in her eyes spellbinding. If I looked too close...

What was I afraid of?

"Of course, Lord Blackstone might object," I said quickly. "Some gentlemen are quite averse to any dogs not of the sporting breed."

Her smile vanished. "My brother will not object," she said rather curtly. She looked at me and seemed more cheerful. "Thank you most kindly for the inspiration, Annalee. I shall make it a top priority to find a suitable puppy..." She let the word trail off to a whisper. "May I call you Annalee? We are to be friends."

Without warning, Victoria Blackstone leaned in, pressed against me and kissed me full on the mouth! And did not stop kissing me. Her lips felt soft and her breath smelled of sweet cloves. For the fleeting seconds, I did not hear the world around me or the strong scent of oranges or the stir of the breeze. There was only the gentle but firm mouth of Victoria upon my own hungry lips and her soft breasts touching my own.

But the voice of reason screamed in my head. Was I insane or so hungry for the lips of a woman that I would risk shame, everything I had worked so hard for?

I pulled away from her, standing unsteady, frozen, staring at her striking green eyes. She stood with an amused smile curling her lips.

"Do not act so shocked, Annalee."

She inched closer again. I could have walked away, run back inside to the safety of the guests. Back to my safe little corner of reality. But I did not. I had to know who this ravishing woman truly was and what she wanted from me.

Her voice was low, intimate. "Annalee, you and I want the same thing, dream the same desires. Let us please not play games, sweet Annalee. I knew you were the same from the moment I laid eyes upon you. Tell me I am wrong."

I looked away from her. I had to. I could not and would not answer her.

"How could you speak to me like this, Miss Blackstone," I asked, sounding foolish and prudish. "You are a Lady, sister to an Earl, Lord Blackstone. I am but hired help."

Her gaze did not leave me. She shrugged her pale beautiful shoulders.

"I am who I am, but we both know that I will never marry a man and you probably won't either."

This woman was beyond bold and yet, I grudgingly found her refreshing and honest. But the situation was dangerous. For me. I straightened my back and stared into her eyes.

"I think it best we both forget this and go back inside."
I wanted nothing more than to run back to Lenore's side.
There was no telling what Miss Wallis and the Earl had
made of her. I ached to feel her beside me, to set my eyes
upon her.

"You are fascinated by Lenore, my sister-in-law."
I was startled by her bold statement. Could this
woman read my mind as well? I could not admit my
feelings for Lenore. Not to Victoria Blackstone. Not to
anyone.

"Miss Blackstone—"

"Victoria, remember?"

"Miss Blackstone," I repeated as sternly as I could
muster, "I will give you my word that I will not mention
this to anyone. You have my word on it. And I beg of you
to do the same. I need my position in Blackstone Castle."

With a grin on her face, she slowly ran her gaze the
length of my body in a very uncomfortable way and then
ran a finger down my cheek.

"Worry not, lovely Annalee, I may be known as Wild
Torri, but I am a very private woman. Take care of Lenore
for me and you shall always have my undying love and
admiration and thanks." She smiled and with a sweeping
motion, pointed to the door into the drawing room. "I
prefer to stay out here awhile longer if you don't mind. It
will take mother longer to think of the orangery to come
looking for me."

I hesitated. Why, I didn't dare ask myself.

"Well, go on," she said in mirth, "Or have you changed
your mind and will keep me company after all?"

*If only you were Lenore, dear God, if only you were
Lenore.*

85

I had to leave. As much as I detested going back into the nest of inequity inside, I feared the magnetic pull of the woman with rich dark hair and fiery green eyes more.

Fifteen

I stepped into the drawing room, my heart still beating rapidly. I inhaled the smell of tobacco and women's sweet fragrances, took a deep breath, exhaled and looked instinctively towards the sofa. I had to clear my head and being near Lenore was the best medicine for that. After all, I was her companion. I should be at her side always.

She was still seated on the couch, but Miss Wallis was now some distance away, standing among a group of young ladies crowding the handsome young Mr. Birnbaum. Already he had the pick of the eligible ladies. I could not keep my thoughts from Victoria. She need not worry about the unwanted attention of Mr. Birnbaum. He was well occupied and the ladies seemed to be in a flurry about something.

I was about to make haste to Lenore's side when the Dowager's voice spoke loudly over the din in the room.

"Miss Wallis has agreed to grace our special guests with a song but needs a good lady to assist with the accompaniment." I saw the Dowager scan the room and preferred to find a hiding space. But she spotted me.

"Miss Stewart, do you not play the pianoforte?" She came excitedly towards me. "Come, dear, we need you to accompany Miss Wallis."

I could not escape. "I do play a little, but I am by no means skilled. I could not submit this fine dinner party to my ineptitude."

"But of course you will," said the Dowager, pointing to the pianoforte.

There was no corner I could hide in. I was caught. I did not wish this limelight and I especially did not wish to play for the coquettish Miss Wallis. Besides, it had been a long time since I had played. But the truth was that once you know how to play the pianoforte, you never really forget.

The pianoforte that sat in the drawing room was a thing of beauty. The rich luster of the deep golden wood and the stark ivory and ebony of the keys and shiny gold trim was inspiring.

Miss Wallis handed me sheet music and I was so thankful that it was a simple song. I took a couple of deep breaths, let them out and began to play. I played the opening bars without striking any wrong notes. The sound was lovely, all the keys in perfect tune.

I had to listen to Miss Wallis in order to follow her, and was surprised at what a well-trained, rich contralto voice she had. I wondered where she'd been trained. Everyone was mesmerized, listening appreciatively to her voice echo through the room.

So much did they love her that when she came to the end of her song, the guests clamored for another. Suddenly, a hand reached out from behind to turn over the music for me. Startled, I glanced behind me to see Victoria Blackstone standing there. And my heart thumped extra beats. How could I forget her lips?

"Thank you," I murmured, and breathed a sigh of relief when instead of singing another song, Miss Wallis protested that she was too tired. She was engulfed by a chorus of applause.

Perfect timing.

I took the moment to run from the pianoforte and prepared my escape to Lenore. But before I barely rose from the embroidered seat, Victoria was at my elbow, two glasses in her hand.

"I thought you might be in need of refreshment after playing so beautifully." Her smile reflected in her eyes.

"Thank you," I said, for a second time. I really could have used the drink and took the glass of dark red from her. Dark red....the color of her hair.

"It's the best of our Sauvignon Reds."

I smiled as I took a deep sip and watched her over the rim. For once, her gaze was preoccupied away from me. She watched Miss Wallis and the Earl who seemed deep in conversation across the room. I wondered what she could be thinking. The relationship between her and her brother seemed strained to say the least. Did she also see a threat in Miss Wallis for the Earl's attention?

I turned to ask if she intended to do anything about the puppy for Lenore, but before I could utter a word, she simply walked away without saying anything more. Victoria Blackstone was an enigma and a puzzling piece in the huge puzzle that was the entire Blackstone family. One thing was certain, however. She knew me. She had guessed where my heart pointed. And what was even more frightening—she suspected my affections for Lenore. I was sure of it.

The dinner party had been a success. Sir Birnbaum and his son John were offered invitations to every castle and manor within miles, including Blackstone.

Lenore appeared nearly asleep on the carriage ride back to the castle and the Earl remained mostly quiet, glancing only once or twice at his exhausted wife and commented on my talented playing of the pianoforte. He offered I could play the pianoforte at the castle anytime I wished.

I was relieved to finally reach Blackstone. My innermost desire was to take Lenore, prepare her for bed and gently lay beside her, watching her take sleep breaths as she rested her head on my chest. But I shook the fantasy clear from my brain and watched as the somber-faced Miss Drake met the Lord and Lenore in the hall and escorted Lenore upstairs as the Earl followed them.

I took a candle from the row standing on the table, lit it and proceeded upstairs to my own bedroom and empty bed. Alone, yet feeling strangely exhilarated. I let my shabby cloak drag to the floor and placed the candle on the drawing closet.

The evening had brought back painful memories, memories I had struggled to efface and now it was time again to face the reality of my daily life. I wasn't a Lady with a closet full of the latest fashion gowns. No, I certainly wasn't that.

I parted the heavy curtain of the window and pressed my face close against the cool glass of the casement. The crescent moon barely cast light upon the park below but instead streaked the landscape with slivers of silver beams. The restlessness inside of me rumbled and the thoughts of the soft and hungry lips of Victoria Blackstone haunted me. I had no feelings for her. I repeated that in my head. My reaction to her kiss was only a physical one borne of my own unmet needs.

How could I sleep tonight? How could I continue to watch Lenore fall apart while her husband dallied with another woman? And what did Victoria want of me that I was willing to give?

Sixteen

The following morning, I dressed quickly, eager and
hopeful of spending time alone with Lenore and putting
the dinner party behind me. Following the nearly magical
feel of the night before, I was desirous to get back into my
day to day life with Lenore. The dinner party had been a
fantasy. In more ways than one.

I should have realized that nothing was routine at
Blackstone Castle by now. The Earl was absent from
breakfast. Lenore mentioned him not and I had no
interest to know his whereabouts. I dared not allow my
thoughts run rampant on that.

Lenore hardly touched her food, a common thing for
her. She seemed to be regressing in the progress she had
made. Her setback had to do with her husband's return. I
believed that with all my heart. I was willing to bet my job
on it. This meant I had to work harder. I would not allow

the negative effects of Lord Blackstone continue to make his wife ill.

She didn't feel strong enough to go outside again this morning and wanted instead to spend her morning in the drawing room catching up on her embroidery. I regretted her decision. Inside the smothering walls of Blackstone, I could not be safe and fully alone with her. Perhaps it was time I should make my feelings more evident and push harder to get her out and about, away from Blackstone.

While she worked quietly at her embroidery, barely looking my way, I busied myself with repair to a tapestry panel of a fire screen.

"How tiresome!"

So engrossed was I in my work, that Lenore's exclamation startled me. I looked up at her.

"Is there something wrong?"

"I've run short of a shade of moss green and now I shall not be able to finish the leaves." She smiled at me warmly. "I may have something suitable in the rosewood box upstairs in my bed chambers. Dear Annalee, perhaps you will fetch it for me?"

Oh, my beating heart, would that I could deny you anything, dear Lenore.

"It is nothing," I said. "I shall be right back."

I put the tapestry panel and the needle with thread and rushed upstairs. Once in her bedchamber, I looked around carefully for the rosewood box and in doing so, noticed the communicating door from Lenore's room to the Earl's room was slightly ajar. Lenore's box was atop a small dresser that stood up against the wall beside the open door.

As I tip toed to it, I heard voices in the Earl's room. Was his valet there? I thought I should be as quiet as I could. As I reached the beautifully carved rosewood box, the voice in the other room stopped me cold. It was Miss Drake.

"My Lord, you must trust me in these matters. You know that my mother knew the ways of plants and what certain potions can do. Your wife can no longer give you a child. Your conscience is clear..."

There was a pause and I stood stone still, fearing to move even a muscle. The Earl's voice was cold, deep.

"And you obviously have none..."

My heart began to thud hard against my chest and I knew I had to get away. I managed my way out of the room, letting out a deep breath. I thought sure any minute I would hear the Earl's voice demanding I stop.

The words I had overheard kept repeating in my head. What were Miss Drake's motives in making such statements to the Earl? And more frightening even was his response. What involvement could the dark Miss Drake have with the Lord of Blackstone? Did she dislike Lenore? I felt a strong disconnect between the two when I first saw them interact. What dark machinations were in motion in Blackstone Castle?

I could not let Lenore know what I had heard. After all, I couldn't make any sense of it really. Not without knowing more. I couldn't sound like a raving madwoman to Lenore. I planned to get to the bottom of things in this castle, no matter how. I would not let harm come to Lenore.

On my way back downstairs, I ran into Lenore, looking glum and in the middle of a big yawn.

"I'm afraid I'm done with embroidery for now." Her eyes twinkled and she smiled as she took my hand. "Will you forgive me for sending you on a useless search for thread?"

How could I be angry?

"Oh, don't be silly, Lenore. I needed the distraction." I could not keep the suspicious conversation from my thoughts.

"I've just exhausted myself and want to lie down for a bit." She let her hand travel up my arm gently, to rest on my shoulder. "Why not take one of those long walks you so love."

I cleared my throat, conscious of the electricity going through my body at her touch. "I do wish you would get out more, Lenore. I strongly suggest you come with me. It might give you some energy."

I knew after I said it that she would not take a walk with me. She seemed drained of energy and this worried me deeply. She shook her head and proceeded up the stairs.

"I promise I shall try harder tomorrow, Annalee."

I watched her go up the staircase and disappear from my sight into the hallway. Now what? I simply had to expend the pent up energy and shake the dark thoughts wracking my body. But I didn't want to leave the castle. Not now. Some part of me felt I had to stay closer than ever to Lenore. Besides, I understood now that it was imperative I keep my ears to the walls inside Blackstone.

Seventeen

I needn't mention that I slept not a wink that night. I lay awake most of the night, tossing and turning, watching the candles burn down and hearing Miss Drake's and the Earl's voices tumble around in my head. It became clear now that my idea of snatching away my dearest Lenore from this dark fortress was not such a crazed plan after all. There was malevolence afoot.

After the night was spent and the intruding fingers of dawn began to pry into my room, I knew that something ill would happen to Lenore if she stayed here. But I had to be careful. Bide my time and remain ever vigilant yet as stealthy as a shadow.

I arose famished this morning. Neither Lenore nor the Earl had come down to supper the night before and I had eaten very lightly in my own room. Dressed in my drab gray dress, I pinned my hair neatly up and readied to race downstairs, hoping to find my Lenore, or at the very least, a big breakfast spread on the table.

Before I pulled the latch on the door, I heard a woman's booming voice downstairs. Good Lord, it sounded like Victoria.

"Hallo, is there no one about in this blasted place?" she boomed again.

I opened the door and heard some other voices join the conversation. I hurried my step. What could be causing the commotion? Was there no rest at this castle? I stopped at the stairs landing.

Sure enough, Victoria Blackstone stood dressed in her usual pantaloons and jacket and hat, a large basket tucked under one arm.

"I will inform the Lady Blackstone that you are here, Miss, but I don't believe she has awakened," stuttered the butler, who was the only other person in the Great Hall.

"No, I will announce myself, thank you," Victoria said quickly, removing her hat and handing it to the flustered butler. "I have a surprise for her that she will welcome being awakened for."

She saw me standing upstairs. I wasn't quite ready to see her again. Her kiss still lingered and confused me.

"Oh, there you are, Miss Stewart." She smiled wide as she ran up the stairs.

"Miss Blackstone..." My voice sounded hoarse and I cleared my throat. "What on earth is all the racket about?" I cast my gaze to the basket, which seemed to be leaning back and forth on its own. I pointed to it. "What do you have in there?"

"I am a woman of my word, you see, Miss Stewart." She held the basket out to me but did not open the top.

She lowered her voice and leaned closer to me. "A puppy. A puppy for Lenore."

Again, she was staring intently at me, a bemused smile on her lips, eyebrows arched. "Have you forgotten that evening at the dinner party already?"

I didn't particular want to indulge her in this conversation at the staircase of Blackstone Castle. Or ever.

"Well, if everyone were still asleep," I said, "I'm certain you've succeeded in waking even the ghosts by now." I wanted so much to look inside the basket at the puppy, but preferred to share the surprise with Lenore. "Come then, let's both wake her up."

We walked swiftly to Lenore's bedchambers. Victoria stepped in front of me and knocked loudly.

"It's Victoria, Lenore, and Miss Stewart's with me. I've got a special surprise for you. It can't wait. Hope you're presentable. We're coming in."

I heard Lenore say something from behind the door, but I could not make out what it was. It mattered not for Victoria flung the door open and I followed behind.

Lenore held what assumed to be her morning cup of hot chocolate to her lips. She put it down quickly when she saw Victoria and me barrel into her room. She wore a pale pink robe of soft satin.

Victoria came to stand in front of the large chair Lenore sat in and placed the basket on the floor. It wiggled.

"A present for you," she announced, and took off the lid to reveal a soft, silky head and two adorable brown eyes.

"A puppy!" cried Lenore. "Oh, the darling creature. Is it for me, Victoria?"

"Yes, if you promise to look after him. Don't feed him too many sugar plums or chocolate and..." She paused, looked at me with a sly grin. "And you must take him for a walk twice a day."

She scooped out the velvety soft spotted puppy, which waddled unsteadily, nose to the floor, toward Lenore. He looked like a brown and white King Charles Spaniel, a favorite among many of the well-to-do families my father and I once entertained. They couldn't bear to leave their Spaniels at home.

Lenore lifted him up and hugged his wiggling body against her. "I shall call him Cyrano and he shall sleep in my sitting room. Miss Drake shall line a special basket for him as a bed."

My heart glowed with warmth. Lenore appeared more animated than at any time since I'd come to Blackstone. Perhaps the puppy had been a stroke of genius by Victoria. I eyed her with admiration and still tasted her lips. I pushed that thought away.

"Well, I leave you two to the charms of Cyrano, then, for I must be in Lustleigh already," Victoria said. She cast a wink at me and walked out as quickly as she'd entered. The woman remained an enigma still.

"Let's take Cyrano for a visit to Mama Blackstone soon," Lenore said, still kissing and squeezing the perky puppy.

I nodded, always ready for a long walk to the Dowager, but not necessarily to see her. It did seem that Cyrano's arrival heralded a step forward for Lenore which I could not have achieved by any other means.

Eighteen

On the pretext of giving Cyrano exercise, Lenore
ventured further afield each day. One bright, cloudless day,
she announced we should walk as far as the Dower House
to display her new puppy. We had a difficult time keeping
up with the bounding Spaniel, and we laughed all the way.

We were out of breath by the time we entered the
salon with Cyrano at Lenore's heels to be surprised that
the Dowager was already entertaining another visitor,
Miss Clarisse Wallis.

As soon as she saw Cyrano, the latter exclaimed: "Oh
what a darling little fellow."

But Cyrano had a different effect on the Dowager. She
frowned.

"Please pick him up, won't you, Miss Stewart, and ask
Ford, the footman, to take him to the stables. I cannot
have a dog's muddy paws in here."

"His paws are not muddy," muttered Lenore, but the Dowager ignored her.

Miss Wallis looked quite ravishing in purple muslin which showed off her hair and complexion to her advantage.

"I am here this morning," she said, "to discuss a fundraising event for the parish with the Dowager Blackstone. And of course, my Lady Blackstone, your help would also be welcome as I was hoping to call on you next at the castle." She smiled sweetly at Lenore.

Like the rattle of a snake, more likely.

"But of course she will," said the Dowager, eyeing Lenore.

"I should like to help, of course, but I would like to discuss it with my husband first."

Good idea to put her off, Lenore. I thought to myself.

"Oh, I have no fear that the Earl will refuse me," said Miss Wallis confidently, "for I had told him of my plans when I met him out riding the other day and he seemed most amiable to the proposition. And he also said he'd not forgotten his promise to show me round Blackstone Castle."

My ears perked up at her words. So she and the Earl had met while riding? Had they been alone? Was it by chance or a planned rendezvous? I could not allow my thoughts and fears to run rampant, but each indiscretion by the Earl led me closer to rationalize my plan to take Lenore away from here and her loveless marriage. But would I be able to heal the hurt that would surely come to my Lenore with such a change of life?

Miss Wallis chattered on while the Dowager regarded her with an indulgent smile. I was, as always, ignored, which I happened to like for it gave me the excellent opportunity to observe the Dowager and Miss Wallis closely. It was evident that the Dowager favored the bold woman. As a matter of fact, I entertained the dangerous notion that she could easily replace Lenore with Miss Wallis if she had her way.

I was thankful that Lenore finally tired of the inane conversation and rose to leave. We said our polite farewells, rescued Cyrano from the stables and began our walk back to the castle. I could see that Lenore was quiet, contemplative. I wanted to hold her hand.

"What do you think of Miss Wallis?"

Her question was unexpected and one I was not sure I should answer honestly and keep my place. Should I really tell the woman I loved how I really felt about that horrid Miss Wallis?

"She is not to my liking in personality, Lenore," I finally said. Inside, I wanted to scream. I was repelled by the woman's crassness and ruthlessness. It was apparent even through her gay chatter. Could I tell Lenore that I believed she had clear designs on the Earl? Was Lenore aware of this?

Lenore, open your eyes, my love.

"I imagine," I continued, "that you must show some amiability in order to appease and oblige the Dowager, but nothing more."

Lenore smiled sweetly at me but her eyes did not smile.

"Yes, I suppose you are right. I must do at least that, though I can never like her." She reached for my hand and my heart thumped in response. She looked at me and giggled slightly. "She didn't really like Cyrano, you know, only pretended."

I laughed and it was nice to hear her laugh with me as we ran to keep up with the racing Cyrano ahead.

It was the last I saw of Lenore or anyone else that night. Blackstone Castle was slowly becoming a tomb. I once again ate a very unsatisfactory supper in my room and paced for part of the night, craving the touch, the feel, the eyes, the essence of Lenore Blackstone, settling for my lumpy bed and blank dreams.

Nineteen

I awoke the following morning to insistent, soft knocking at my door. Wiping the sleep from my eyes and slipping my robe on, I nearly stumbled to open the door.

Betsy stood there, wringing her hands and a worried look on her face.

"Pardon me, Miss, but the Lady Blackstone is asking to see you. Miss Drake has gone into town with the Lord Blackstone and the Lady is requiring your presence, she says, Miss."

I yawned and wondered exactly where and why those two had gone so early.

"Did Miss Drake tell you where she was going and why?"

Betsy shook her head quickly. "No, Miss, they just left word they were going into Bath and would not be back until the next morn."

Bath? And they wouldn't be back until tomorrow? That meant I had Lenore all to myself for the entire day. This could prove interesting and to my advantage. I waved her off with a smile. "Very well, Betsy, I'll dress and get to Lady Blackstone right away." Poor Betsy scampered away like a harried rabbit. Of course, I wanted nothing more than to meet Lenore. I was alone, well, not counting the staff which was sparse and hardly around, with Lenore. And she wanted to see me.

I dressed quickly, letting my hair loose beyond my shoulders and nearly ran to Lenore's room. I knocked twice gently.

"Lenore, it's Annalee." I opened the door without waiting for a reply.

She stood in front of one of the huge windows, the cup of chocolate in one hand. The drapes were pulled back and the sun cast rays of bright morning light that played like golden fingers upon her skin. She wore a very sheer, revealing, low neck gown. I struggled to keep from not staring at her beauty, for I was besotted with desire for her. She glowed like a goddess.

Her face beamed when I came into the room, I was struck dumb by her glory.

"Oh, dear Annalee, always here at my beck and call." Her voice and eyes teased.

I had to tear my gaze from her or she would surely have thought me nothing more than a lecherous woman and run me out of her house. I lowered my head and stared at the floor.

"But that is one of my duties, you know, Lenore."

She said nothing and I forced my eyes back up to her. She stood contemplating me with a wistful smile.

"Oh, but you are more than that, my Annalee..." She paused and walked slowly to where I stood. She was close enough to where I could see her breasts rise and fall with the rhythm of her breathing, ever so gently, ever so lovely.

"Since you arrived, Annalee, there has been a compelling attraction between us, a deep bond and mutual desire for each other's welfare—" She stopped and without hesitation, took my hand slowly and held it. "Annalee, you have spoken always with respect and restraint, I know, but genuine care..." Again, she paused and stepped even closer.

For that instant, standing in her private bed chambers, Blackstone Castle was so quiet, so still, that I believed Lenore and I were alone in another world, place and time. I did not let go of her hand. No, I knew the time had come for honesty and proclamations of my love for her. She was saying the same thing, in her own, shy, gentle way. This was a woman married to the Lord Blackstone, an Earl. Professing attraction or worse, love, for another, let alone a woman, could mean total ruination, or worse. But today, alone in Blackstone Castle, I felt we had reached a point where there was no turning back. No return.

Her large, bewitching blue eyes held me spellbound. If only I could have jumped into the ocean of blue in her eyes and drowned I would have done so willingly. Lenore took a sip of her chocolate, all the while holding her gaze on me over the rim of the cup. But she tipped the cup too quickly and spilled some of the dark, rich chocolate on the edge of her gown over her breasts.

I watched, seduced by the slow dance of the chocolate down her bosom and below. The heat building through my insides was a raging inferno, a fire I had not enough restraint to dowse.

I took the cup from her hand, placed it quickly on the table and drew her swiftly to me. I looked into her eyes, seeking either disgust and withdrawal or approval. I found the same fever that burned in mine. I leaned in and licked gently at the dribble of chocolate that had spilled upon her chest. The chocolate tasted somewhat bitter. Was it dark chocolate? With increasing hunger, I worked my tongue into the rim of her gown and finished lapping the chocolate from her skin.

"Oh, my God, Annalee," she whispered hoarsely, "could this be—"

I kissed her deeply, stopping her words, as I slipped the stained gown from her shoulders. She did not move away or push me from her, but held my face softly in her hands, her eyes searching mine.

"My darling Annalee, you must never leave me now, you know?" She sounded so pleading.

"You and I, my Lenore, will go away, far away, to another continent if we must, but we shall be together forever. Nothing and no one will separate us now."

I was vaguely aware of the door and wondered if I had latched it, but the volcano erupting within my belly didn't care if one of the servants opened that door and discovered us. It didn't matter anymore. I was blind to any danger. I only wanted to satisfy the desire bursting from within.

I urgently began to remove my own dress while leading Lenore toward her bedroom. She clung to me, unbuttoning the back of my dress for me as we moved. I undid all the pins from her hair, the golden tresses falling below her naked shoulders.

I sat her gently on the bed and swept off the last of my garments. We were both now bare to each other, body and soul. I could not help but notice how thin and pale she was, but her skin glowed like fine china, her breasts, rising and falling rapidly now, small but perfect, nipples a deep brown and erect. Waiting for my mouth.

I pulled her close and laid her gently down into the voluminous pillows that were sprawled across her bed. As I ran my hands through her fine hair, I was filled with a joy that was impossible for me to understand. I looked down upon the woman who I'd known was fated to be mine.

She smiled, her eyes wide with desire. "How have you come to love me, darling Annalee, I am but a sick woman."

I shook my head, finding it hard to find my voice.

"You are only sick because no one has loved you. Oh, my dearest Lenore, can you not see it? I am drowning in the sea of you," I whispered as I leaned in closer. Lenore's lips, inches from mine, were like the soft pink petals of a fully opened rose. "And I have no desire for a lifesaver."

I kissed her, fiercely. Her mouth was soft, full and she tasted of chocolate. I pulled her close, our bodies as one. She wrapped her arms around me and pulled me in even closer. She smelled of sunshine and citrus. Her scent aroused me as I pushed my face into the mass of her hair and then worked my way down her neck, taking nibbles of one ear. She met my lovemaking with increasing abandon, leaning back into her pillows, eyes closed, grasping the delicate pillowcases in her fists and meeting my lips with her body.

Taking one of her breasts in my hand, I brought my mouth to her hard nipple, licking and then taking it all into my mouth. Sounds of ecstasy escaped her lips and I felt the ache between my thighs pounding. With one knee,

I separated her legs apart and continued down the soft, silky skin of her stomach and belly with my tongue.

Lenore arched up and one knee came between my legs and I could not control the loud moan of uncontrolled desire rise from my throat. I wanted, needed to pleasure my Lenore above all else. I slipped down, between her legs and placed my fingers through her soft hair and into her wetness, Lenore arched up to meet my hand, reaching swiftly and suddenly guiding my hand inside her. Her head fell back deep into her pillow, her eyes closed, her whole body pushing against me.

When I put my tongue to the river that was her, Lenore screamed and grabbed for me, expending herself completely. I felt myself explode with rapture, a total epiphany of sexual joy. Was such completeness possible?

Spent and exhausted from our lovemaking, we both lay in each other's arms. Lenore began to shake and I held her even tighter, running my hand through her hair and placing soft kisses on her lips and neck.

"My darling Lenore, you are safe now, forever. We belong to each other. I will love you always, my sweet," I whispered into her ear.

She looked at me, tears dripping down her cheeks.

"Annalee, heart of mine, what you said about no one loving me..." She paused and I feared she was going to break down, but instead, a smile of bliss formed on her lips. "You were right. I'm afraid I've been romancing death more than anyone of flesh and blood—"

"No," I said softly, putting a finger to her lips. "Don't stay such things, darling. You mustn't speak thus. It is destructive and serves no Godly purpose thinking such thoughts. I will never leave you and I have more love than you will need or want in a lifetime. I will not let you down and I will love you always. Give me a chance to show you that my love will protect us both."

She rested her head on my shoulder and sighed, running her hand over my lips. I believed and meant everything I said to my beloved Lenore. What still frightened me and what I could not control were the repercussions and the destruction that was sure to follow from Foster Blackstone and the entire Blackstone family. And the memory of Victoria Blackstone and that night of a sudden kiss suddenly became distant and frivolous.

Twenty

Knocking. Again. This time, I opened my eyes with alarm. Lenore lay quietly beside me, wrapped tight in my arms, her mass of golden hair spilling over me. Lovemaking. I remembered. I smiled while quietly disengaging from the frail arms of my Lenore. It had been real. Not a dream. But someone was knocking and calling out for Lenore outside the chamber door. Good thing I had locked it after all before Lenore and I had made passionate love.

"Lady Blackstone? Miss Stewart?" It was Betsy. Again.

Lenore stirred from sleep and looked at me, her blue eyes wide with confusion. I put a finger to my lips and smiled.

"Shh. I'll take care of Betsy. Dress quickly, love."

I called out as I picked up the scattered slip and dress from the floor and began to awkwardly button myself as I moved to the door.

"I'll be right there, Betsy." I said loud enough so she heard.

I ran to Lenore, my back to her. "Button me, my darling. Hurry." When she finished the last button, I turned around and placed a quick kiss upon her lips so soft. "I love you furiously." I held her for a few seconds longer. "Now, go grab a cloth and put it upon your brow and sit down deep into your chair in your chamber. And don't say a word. You've had a horrid headache and I've been...ministering to you." I couldn't suppress the smile and a wink.

My poor, sweet Lenore was flustered and a bit frightened, I could tell, but did exactly what I told her to do. I smoothed out one of the many creases in my dress and opened the door.

Betsy stood wringing her hands, a harried look in her eyes.

"Pardon me, Miss, but the Dowager Blackstone is downstairs raising a storm, she is, wondering why no one ever meets her at the door besides the butler."

"I was tending to Lady Blackstone's headache this morning and heard nothing." A white lie like that would surely hurt no one.

Betsy barely cast a look at Lenore who was definitely playing the part.

"The Dowager, Miss, she doesn't like to be kept waiting."

"Fine, Betsy," I said, "Go back down and inform the Dowager that Lady Blackstone will be right down."

I watched her scamper away. With Betsy gone, I wondered what the old woman could possibly want so early in the morning. What if there was an emergency? No,

Victoria would have come galloping down on her horse. But what if Victoria was the emergency?

Lenore had removed the rag from her forehead and gotten up.

"Darling, your mother-in-law is downstairs." I wrapped her into my arms tight. She was such a perfect fit.

"Good heavens, Annalee, what could she want?"

"I haven't the foggiest, but you'd best get presentable and hurry downstairs or she will come up here to fetch you."

Before taking off to her bedroom, she kissed me sweetly, softly and took a nibble of my ear. Was it all a dream? I was still dreaming. That was it. I smiled broadly, hardly able to understand the complete joy and light filling my very being. And yet, the dark shadows of fear still dwelled in the corners of my mind. What now of our relationship? Had I put undue stress upon my dearest? Her relations with her husband had been a disaster from the start and had grown colder...harder.

And now dangerous.

What if I had put her in real danger? If the Lord Blackstone ever found out, what would he do? What was he capable of? And what of his mother? And Victoria? Victoria. I shivered, even though it was quite warm in Lenore's chambers.

My stomach tightened with concerns that had no place following the love shared hours ago. What of my place now in Lenore's life? Would I be content to take a mere companion role in her daily routine as if nothing had happened? Did I really have a place in her reality now that my fantasy had been fulfilled?

The Dowager was in a downright nasty mood. I could tell by the squared shoulders and flaring nostrils. As usual, she offered me a look of disdain as both Lenore and I greeted her in the sitting hall. Her smile was as contrite as she could manage.

"Good Lord, child, why must I always be met by the lowest of your staff each and every visit? You should be up and about, especially walking that beastly little dog of yours."

"Good morning, Mama," Lenore said, feigning a light kiss on the cheek of her mother-in-law. "Since Foster and Miss Drake are away, I thought to..." she paused and snuck a quick look at me, "...sleep the morning."

I hid the uncontrollable smile inside. Sleep indeed.

The Dowager Blackstone glared at her. "Well, I don't know if Foster has told you, but after you and Miss Stewart left the other day, Miss Wallis and I agreed upon the most perfect fundraiser for the church parish."

She let the statement trail off, expecting our supposed excitement for the surprise. But neither Lenore nor I especially cared one bit what she and the dreadful Miss Wallis had devised for their dreary fundraiser.

The older lady finally gave up and smiled proudly.

"Blackstone Castle is to host a charity Masquerade Ball."

Just what we needed, another party. I groaned inside.

Her smile faded when it became obvious that neither of us was as excited as she.

"Well, Lenore, this will give Blackstone Castle a chance to shine and come alive once more and an opportunity for you to make Foster proud."

114

I would gladly have slapped her for Lenore, but held myself from speaking. Just because Lenore and I had made fierce love this very morning did not entitle me to be that big a part of her life. Not at all.

Lenore reached out and placed a hand on the Dowager's arm.

"Oh, a Masquerade Ball sounds wonderful and mysterious, but I should consult with Foster first—"

"But do you not speak with your husband at all?" asked the old woman incredulously. "He has already agreed. Why do you think he and Miss Drake have gone to Bath? They've gone to have costumes made, fabrics for new Castle hangings, food and party favors ordered. He is very supportive of Miss Wallis's desire to help her father and the parish." She paused, eyeing Lenore. "You would have no objection, would you Lenore?"

"I? Oh no," stammered Lenore, obviously taken aback.

The Dowager snorted. "We intend to invite many privileged couples who will donate generously to the fund. Only the ballroom here at the Blackstone would hold so many invited guests."

The old woman knew poor Lenore had been bullied by her own husband, Miss Wallis and herself into such a large ball. There was nothing Lenore could do but graciously accept...or run away with me.

One dream come true at a time. Let's not get greedy.

"You must not fear being inconvenienced," continued the Dowager, "The Dean will engage additional servants to cope with the extra work involved." She stopped and looked perplexed at Lenore.

"But I do not understand how Foster does not communicate these things to his own wife."

Lenore lowered her head, avoiding the badgering stare of the Dowager.

"He rarely confides his movements to me."

Oh, how I wished to shove this interfering and wicked old woman out the door, but instead, I cleared my throat. It was all I could do.

The Dowager glanced at me as if I were a pesky fly she wished to swat away and simply ignored me.

"Well, once Foster and Miss Drake return, please be so good as to ask him to call on me." She moved away but glanced back. "You won't forget, will you?

Lenore smiled sweetly. "No, Mama, of course I won't."

Oh, my Lenore, I will teach you so many things, but first, how to get a backbone.

Twenty One

We spent the day blissfully ignorant of both Miss Drake and Lord Blackstone and of the staff at the castle.

Although I ached to spend most of the time in bed, wrapped around the body of Lenore, she appeared full of new-found energy and expressed a desire to walk Cyrano, who had been restless.

I wished to go back down to the river's edge below and investigate the odd tower and boat tethered to it, but Lenore turned her lovely nose at the idea. She really didn't like the rippling waters of Blackheart River.

We compromised for a short walk in the gardens to wood's edge if I could make passionate love to her behind the closed doors of her room. It turned out to be a marvelous time walking and running with Cyrano. The air was clear and crisp and the sun bright. But I had a hard time concentrating on anything but Lenore's soft, smooth creamy skin beneath my fingers and the way she moved against me when I pleasured her.

But something that pleased me the most was the vigor in her energies and the color in Lenore's cheeks. While I wanted to take full credit for that, I wondered why her moods and rise and fall of her health were so erratic. What was the catalyst that sent her spiraling to her dark spaces and illness?

Just past the mid morning table treat of two baskets full of assorted fruits, Lenore came up with a most delicious idea. She asked James, one of the grooms, to bring about the large tin bathtub to her room. It was quite an ordeal, and we could hardly control our giggles as we watched James and the other groom bring up the tub. They set it in the middle of the room, with a large, rather grimy tarp beneath it as to spare the expensive rug from spillover.

Although she had called it a large tub, it was hardly that. Well, to my eyes anyway. Would the both of us fit? My whole body quivered in anticipation of luxuriating in a real bath. I hadn't soaked in a bathtub since leaving my privileged life. And of course, languishing in a tub filled with soap and Lenore would be a heaven I hardly felt I deserved.

Shortly after the grooms left, Betsy and one other maid came and filled the tub with hot, steaming water, each carrying two buckets at a time. Lenore had disappeared into her bedroom, whispering that she must get ready, whatever that meant. I wished that I could help poor Betsy and the other girl bring up the hot water, for they labored so, but I knew they wouldn't allow me.

Betsy came up one more time with one bucket, since the tub was nicely full. She left me holding a bar of square soap and big bath sponge and rushed off with sweating brows. She should be rewarded with a bath herself, I thought. The steaming water looked so inviting, with fingers of misty heat dancing in the air above the hot water. If Lenore did not hurry, I would steal her bath all to myself.

She came from her bedroom, wrapped in a silk robe of the most vivid color of Plum I had ever seen, her blonde hair arranged neatly atop her head.

"I thought the water would go cold waiting for you," I teased.

She ignored me and instead, walked slowly to each of the large windows in the living chamber and pulled the drapes on each one. I was beginning to like this bath idea more and more.

"Light the candles, darling," she said as she closed the final drapes, leaving only a sliver of sunshine in the room for me to take one of the burning candles and light each and every candle in her room.

When the last candle was burning bright, Lenore pulled the final drape. The room was ablaze with candlelight. She came to stand before me, smiling coyly.

"I thought you'd be ready to get in the bath."

I looked at the tub again. "Will the both of us fit, do you think?"

Without a word, she dropped the robe to the floor in one quick movement and stood in all her glory before me.

"Now, my Annalee, shall you bathe with me?"

I had another worry besides the size of the tub.

"And you're certain neither the Earl nor Miss Drake have the key to these chambers?" I valued my life and had plans for my future. Yes, I had locked all the doors to

Lenore's chambers, but I did not wish to die in a steamy bathtub at the end of a sword or a blast from a pistol!

She cocked her head of blonde curls to one side and arched a delicate eyebrow. "Of course, dearest, have I not told you that neither myself nor the Earl have keys to the rooms in the castle? Only Mrs. Patterson holds the keys to Kingdom, so to speak." Lenore smiled at me, obviously pleased with her witty retort.

She began to unbutton my dress while kissing me softly. I felt the heat build inside. I stripped the last of my undergarments into a messy pile at my feet and reached out for her, but she pulled away, instead slipping leisurely, teasing me with her gaze, into the hot water of the tub.

Lenore leaned up against one end of the tub and raised a hand to me.

"Come, plenty of room for you." Her blue eyes caught the flicker of the candlelight, gold hair shimmering. "And bring the Castile soap with you," she said with a grin.

She'd been right. I slipped in on the other side of the tub and sat down, knees bent, back against the tub, facing Lenore, our legs straddling each other. The steam still rising from the hot water left a mist of warm heat on our faces. It was a tight fit, but oh-so-perfect for me to just reach over.

Without any words spoken, I lathered up the soap until the big, puffy sponge was fully lathered and began to rub across her breasts, one at a time. She leaned her head back, eyes closed, mouth open. The soap was creamy and left her skin smooth, soft like velvet.

Rinsing off her soapy breasts, I could not help myself from leaning over further and put my mouth upon one wet breast. It tasted slightly of olive oil. My hand took her other breast and bit hard on the now fully erect nipple. The sound of ecstasy escaped from Lenore's open mouth.

"Oh, my God, my Annalee, you have awakened such wild desire in me I never even dreamed," she said in a raspy, low voice.

What cared I that we were in water and in a cramped bathtub. I wanted to pleasure Lenore over and over, in everyway and anywhere our desires took us. Yes, this was the best bath of my life!

I continued to rub the soapy sponge under the water, over all her body, traveling to below and between her legs. I no longer had use for the sponge, so I let it float to the top and began to rub swiftly using my fingers. Lenore moved to my lovemaking, the water spilling over the sides. I pushed inside her, moving forward as far as I could. Her fingers grasping the edge of the bathtub grew white as she stifled a short but controlled scream of orgasm. Household staff engaged in unhealthy rumors in every household and we wished not to give anyone at Blackstone Castle ammunition for ugly talk.

Getting up and on my knees was going to be hard, I knew, but I did it, causing a great deal of water to go over the tub and onto the tarp the grooms had placed over the carpet. It mattered little as I needed to be on her, to feel her satisfaction. It was awkward but after a bit of maneuvering, I finally got turned around and lay with my back to her, my head resting on her chest.

I thought this a fitting finale to our love-making—both soaking contentedly, eyes closed and the water still after our sojourn to ecstasy. But then Lenore began to whisper softly in my ears—words of love and tender longings. I gazed up to look at her when I felt a gentle, slow circular movement between my legs. I wouldn't have imagined such slight motion could have the effect it did until I felt Lenore's fingers open me to her more insistent and rhythmic rubbing. I arched my back and clinched my muscles. My left leg found purchase on the floor of the tub, but my right leg slipped and shot up through the water and sent the sponge flying. It didn't matter; I was oblivious to all that as Lenore continued to make love to me with her words and her body until she brought me to final release.

After sweet moments of her gentle kisses and her lips caressing my face, we heard a small hissing sound. Glancing at the fireplace, we both noticed the sponge on the mantle above. Dripping.

"My dear Annalee, that's quite a kick you have, my love," said Lenore, laughing. "Quite a kick indeed."

We both had a good laugh and Lenore giggled endearingly, but the look on her face was one of triumph, unexpected, even to herself, perhaps, but certain nonetheless. It brought great joy in my heart to see this new, bold and awakened Lenore. But would happen when the dark presence of her husband and Miss Drake came back into our lives?

As the water cooled and candles flickered, we each knew our time of pleasure and being together alone would soon end. We both knew that once the Earl and Miss Drake returned the next morning, we would have only memories to fill our days until I could take Lenore away from Blackstone Castle, forever and far, far away. With this knowledge, our warm kiss in the cooling water was all the more tender.

Twenty Two

It was our last loving moment together.

I was awake early the next morning when the Earl and Miss Drake arrived back to the castle. There was a big commotion below. My heart and my mind were on Lenore. Was she still asleep or did she even get much sleep? Would she kiss her husband with a hunger as she kissed me? I knew that answer. She loved him not and he did not love her. There was only play acting. That, at least, pleased me.

But how could I continue to live here with Lenore as merely a companion and never again touch her skin, smother her with kisses or make her call my name with abandon in the throws of lovemaking? It was as I feared. The boundary line should never have been crossed. Lovers we were never meant to be. She was the wife of Lord Foster Blackstone. She was his property as surely as this castle of stone and wood was.

I dressed, devoid of any enthusiasm for anything but to see Lenore. I wondered if when I entered Lenore's chambers, the memories of the hours, the day, spent there would be too overwhelming. But I had to see her. I was, after all, her companion.

I knocked once and entered, without waiting for a response. The large room was quiet, the sun coming through the large windows spread rays of light and touched everything in the room. I did not see Miss Drake and that was a big relief. But when I saw Lenore, my heart sank.

She sat deep into her favorite chair, surrounded by pillows, looking pale and forlorn. It was too much like the Lenore I had first met when I arrived at Blackstone Castle that fateful day.

"Lenore," I said in a low voice, still wondering if the dour and dark Miss Drake might be lurking somewhere.

Her face brightened when she saw me and she got up, coming to fling her arms around me.

"Oh, I'm so happy you've come."

I noticed that she'd already had her morning chocolate. I remembered how odd it had tasted on my tongue.

She sat back down and I sat on the floor beside her, my hands on her lap. I picked up the empty cup.

"I must say, Lenore, I don't know how you have a taste for this horrid chocolate. It tastes like no chocolate I've ever had."

She looked at me and the cup. "I wouldn't mind tea with cream, really, but Miss Drake swears the chocolate is a family recipe that helps with what ails me and will give me more spirit and verve."

More like saps the spirit from you with the odd taste.

124

I couldn't but wonder why Miss Drake would have Lenore drink something that was obviously not beneficial at all but seemed to drain her more than provide anything to lift my love from whatever ailed her.

My mind went back to the ominous conversation I'd overheard between the Earl and Miss Drake.

"My Lord, you must trust me in these matters. You know that my mother knew the ways of plants and what certain potions can do. Your wife can no longer give you a child. Your conscience is clear..."

I nearly dropped the cup to the floor so distraught were my thoughts. The evil that was forming in my mind could not be possible. How easy could it be for someone versed in plants and their medicinal...or venomous qualities...to poison food or drink? But what purpose would Miss Drake have to cause harm to Lenore? And where did the Earl fit into the foul picture? If he no longer wanted Lenore, it would be easy to divorce her and cast her out of Blackstone.

I took my dear Lenore's hand. "Darling, how long have you been drinking your chocolate?"

"Not long after I..." She paused but a brief moment. "Not long after I lost my child in the miscarriage. I didn't want to refuse because she seemed so positive it would help by drinking the chocolate each morning."

I smiled tightly, trying to control the churning in my stomach. "It hasn't helped, love. I believe the fresh air and Cyrano have had better results." I had to get her to stop drinking the foul tasting drink until I could find a way to see what, if anything, harmful was in it.

Lenore looked at me, her blue eyes locked on mine. "Should I stop drinking it?" Her eyebrow arched in question. "Do you suspect something in the chocolate might be making me ill?"

I squeezed her hand. "Why not tell Miss Drake that you wish to have tea and cream for your morning drink instead of the chocolate for a change."

"And if she insists on the chocolate?"

Oh, my Lenore, you are but a trusting child still.

"Insist that you will not drink the chocolate. It has done nothing for you."

Cyrano suddenly came bouncing from the bed chamber and flung himself at me. I hugged him and patted his ears. Lenore laughed and it was an uplifting sound in the deathly quiet room, but it was suddenly interrupted by a deep cough. Lenore put a hand up to her mouth. I had not heard her cough like that before.

"My darling," I said firmly, "you must promise me that you will insist to Miss Drake that you do not wish to have the chocolate but want tea instead."

She stifled another small cough but smiled at me.

"I will be as forceful as I can."

I was a woman with a plan. I knew my sweetest Lenore was not a strong woman. She would certainly give it her best to stand up to Miss Drake but would shrivel to the woman's over-bearing power over her. Because I knew that, I had to take care of things on my own and in my own way.

Lenore didn't care that I took the cup with the remnants of chocolate still lacing the inside. Obviously, there was no one I trusted within Blackstone. There was only one person that came close to earning my trust and I had no real reason to give her that trust. Only my inner instinct guided me. Victoria Blackstone might be the only person that might be able to help.

It would be a gamble to take the cup to her and ask if she knew of anyone in Lustleigh competent in poisons that could test what was in the cup. It was the only way to allay my fears that Lenore was being poisoned. Perhaps Miss Drake really was adding a medicinal ingredient strictly for beneficial purposes and all with good intent but why could I not believe that? I had to be sure.

I had no idea whether Miss Blackstone was home at Dower House, but I used taking Cyrano out for a walk as an excuse to leave the castle and Lenore's side. I was thankful I ran neither into Miss Drake or the Earl before embarking.

Cyrano as always made the walk an adventure. I had to sometimes chase him out of the woods after he took off after a rabbit, but it had dawned a day bright with sun and free of clouds in a clear blue sky, as clear and blue as the eyes of my beloved Lenore.

I had no idea what would await me at the Dowager's house and expected to be berated or ignored or worse. But I must still have been in the Good Lord's graces, for I was informed by the butler who answered the door that the Dowager was in town with Miss Wallis finalizing plans for the Masquerade Ball.

"I'm here to see Miss Blackstone, please." I had cradled Cyrano in my arms and held on tight to him. I was not about to allow him to be put in the stables again.

My insides were like a thick jelly. I knew it was presumptuous of me to come knocking on the Dowager's door without an invitation and without Lenore or the Earl. I thought certain the butler would direct me to the servant's entrance out back. But he merely seemed confused with proper etiquette for the likes of me. When he heard I had come to call on Victoria, he seemed relieved.

"Yes, Miss, Miss Blackstone is upstairs in her apartment. Whom shall I say is calling?" He eyed Cyrano with some discomfort.

"Miss Annalee Stewart. She will want to hear me out, I assure you."

I didn't feel as secure as I pretended to the butler.

To my surprise, he ushered me inside and asked that I wait in the sitting room while he closed the two doors behind him and disappeared. Being here brought back memories of a dinner party that seemed so long ago and a kiss. I smiled, for I could not deny the irony and sweetness in that evening. Victoria Blackstone had professed attraction and interest in me, never suspecting in her wildest dreams that I was in love with her sister-in-law.

My wistful thoughts were interrupted by the sound of the doors slowly opening. Cyrano squirmed in my arms. Victoria stood there, a look of surprise and amusement on her face.

"This is indeed a surprise, Miss Stewart..." she paused. "...Annalee. I rushed downstairs when I heard Torrance say you were waiting in the sitting room...alone."

"Well, not exactly alone," I laughed as Cyrano jumped away and ran towards Victoria, who patted him and ran her hands over his fur.

"Lenore has properly trained him, I assume?" She looked at me as Cyrano licked her hands and wagged his tail affectionately.

"He will be fine until our walk back to the castle," I said. "He took care of his...business on the way here."

Cyrano took off to investigate the room, his nose close to the ground, sniffing for anything interesting. Victoria stood smiling, her gaze as intense as the rays of the sun filtering through the large windows. I couldn't help but notice her bagging pantaloons, light boots and full sleeved blouse. Two buttons remained undone down her chest, revealing minimal cleavage. Why was I drawn to her? I wondered if she had rushed to meet me in the middle of dressing. How did she get away with dressing so manly? Surely, the talk of the town could not be positive. Already they had nicknamed her Wild Torri. What else did they whisper behind the backs of the Blackstones?

I shook my thoughts away from her. I had urgent business with Victoria and not fanciful ruminations.

"I was afraid I would miss you..." I paused and smiled. "Although I must admit to being quite relieved that I missed the Dowager."

She walked slowly toward me, taking a glance at Cyrano who had tuckered himself out and found a nice spot near a chair to relax.

"Shall I guess what brings you here, then, Annalee?" She stopped and smiled wide. "But that might not be what you wish to entertain."

I cleared my throat. It was too late to change my mind now.

"I'm afraid it is neither play nor whim that brings me here...Victoria." It felt inappropriate saying her name, yet easy at the same time. "I fear for Lenore and I need your help. You are the only person I felt I could trust. I pray you will not let me down." I had no time but to get to the heart of the matter.

She needed to see the honesty in my eyes. I met her eyes with my own intense gaze. The smile on her face turned to a worried frown. Her green eyes filled with concern.

"For God's sake, Annalee, what is it? Is Lenore in trouble? Is she ill?"

I looked away, still unsure if she might think me mad once I told her what my suspicions were and who I implicated. After all, I had no proof. But that was why I needed her help.

I reached out and put a hand on her arm.

"I beg of you not to think me mad or foolish until I finish telling you everything."

She eyed my hand on her shoulder and looked back at me.

"Annalee, you are one of the sanest women I've met in some time. And I know you want the best for Lenore."

Inside, the butterflies in my stomach settled into a gentle flutter and I took a deep breath before continuing.

"That's just it, I don't know. I am to assume that you know Lenore has been drinking a chocolate each morning..." I paused, wondering how much Victoria actually knew.

She nodded. "Yes, I've visited several times and seen Lenore drinking her chocolate in the morning."

"It's something Miss Drake is forcing her to drink," I continued. "She is adding some sort of family recipe to the chocolate that will help Lenore get better. But that's the problem. She hasn't really improved at all."

"Forcing?" Victoria's brows furrowed.

"Well, she insists that Lenore drink it, despite the fact that Lenore prefers tea and cream."

Victoria suddenly walked away and stood, her back to me, facing the large windows.

"Has Lenore made her wishes known to Miss Drake?"

"I've urged her to make it clear to Miss Drake that she will no longer have the chocolate and that tea and cream should be substituted instead."

She walked back to me and took both my hands in hers, her gaze set upon me. "And we both know that our dear Lenore doesn't have a strong voice of her own." Her hands were warm, strong.

"I will add my voice to hers and stand up to Miss Drake if I must. Lenore is not alone in this."

Victoria looked deeper into my eyes. "But something else troubles you. Something more brings you to me."

The nearness of her was distracting and that was troublesome to me. Why? Was it the lie I had to tell her?

"I accidentally tipped over her nearly empty cup one morning on her table and took a taste of the chocolate. It had a most unpleasant aftertaste. It sat heavy on my tongue. Too bitter. It's no wonder Lenore sickens." I turned my nose up at the memory of the foul taste.

"Could it be that whatever Miss Drake is using is just simply a bitter herb, then?"

I could not keep the conversation between her brother, the Earl, and Miss Drake from Victoria. She had to know. I relayed the entire conversation without adding my own deeply disturbing conclusions but could not leave out my questioning of why such a conversation and what could it mean.

Without waiting, I handed her the cup I had brought in my reticule with the traces of the chocolate.

"What would it hurt to have someone well versed in such things in Lustleigh tell us what exactly is in the chocolate?" I looked her squarely in those deep green eyes. "It would be of great relief to me and I think you too, Victoria."

She took the cup and without saying a word, walked to the chair where Cyrano lay sleeping below on the carpet and sat deep down into the chair, looking down at the cup.

Had I gone too far? Would she think me breaking a trust by repeating a private conversation between the Earl and Miss Drake? I feared her silence and the absence of her gaze upon me.

She finally reached down to run a hand down Cyrano's back and looked up at me.

"You're to go back to Blackstone and not say a word to Lenore or anyone else." Victoria got up suddenly, walked to the two double doors, and then turned back to me. "You've done well putting your trust in me, Annalee. I will send word to you by one of my own trusted grooms when I have the answers we seek." She looked at the cup. "Go now. I'm sure Lenore will be missing you."

I grabbed Cyrano who was still groggy from his sleep and walked quickly out the doors. Victoria smiled a crooked smile and closed the doors behind me. But it was not a glad parting.

I left, moving quickly toward the path through the woods. The cold icy look in her eyes frightened me. What had I done?

Twenty Three

I arrived at the castle flustered and with concern over the length of time I'd spent away. If anyone had spied me and kept track, I had just taken Cyrano for a near hour and half walk!

As I hurried up the stairs, Cyrano firmly in my arms, I nearly ran into Lord Blackstone.

"Pardon, Lord Blackstone, but Cyrano has gotten the most vigorous exercise and I was on the way to Lady Blackstone's room for some water." I hoped I sounded convincing and that he would not noticed my flushed cheeks and heavy breathing.

He stood gazing at me with an amused yet cool and detached air. Did he believe me? Had he known when I left and how long I'd been gone? He finally smiled slightly, eyeing Cyrano with some annoyance.

"I fail to understand why Lenore keeps such a little dog. She barely cares for it herself and it is useless to me as a hunting dog." When he looked at me, his eyes softened. "Well, go on then. Lenore has been impatient for you."

Lenore. Her name from his lips sounded sullied, somehow tainted and cheap. Something about him made my stomach churn and an uncomfortable feeling run up my spine.

I wanted to run, but instead slightly bowed and took my leave, rushing to Lenore's room. I made the mistake of assuming she was alone in her room and rushed inside without knocking or announcing myself. I had to be more careful, for I found Lenore standing in the middle of her parlor, splendid in a medieval style gown with puffy sleeves and low cut neckline and high, stiff collar. Miss Drake was bent near the floor, pinning the hem.

I stopped where I stood, aware of the glare from Miss Drake. But I cared not for the sour Miss Drake because the joy that glowed from Lenore's smile and azure eyes lifted my heart. She loved me. I knew it then for certain. It was the look of love.

"Pardon me, Miss Drake, Lady Blackstone. I didn't knock..." I faltered, but remembered Cyrano who squirmed in my arms, wanting to bolt free and run to Lenore. "Cyrano and I took a very long walk and we are both thirsty and worn out I'm afraid. I wanted to get him to his water."

I knew I had to tear myself away from the vision of Lenore in her Masquerade costume, for I could not stand there like a fool girl in love, gaping lovingly at her lover with a dog in her arms. Miss Drake eyed me with the gaze of a predator bird as I briskly took Cyrano into Lenore's bed chamber where his own bed and water bowl waited.

I left him lapping up as much water as his poor little tongue could handle and heard Lenore fussing at Miss Drake as I walked back into the sitting parlor.

"This will be fine," she said with a roll of bright blue eyes. "This isn't some grand ball in the King's Castle, only a charity ball for the parish." Her brows furrowed in frustration.

When she saw me, her face softened. "Come, Miss Stewart, we shall discuss your garb for the ball." She beckoned with both her arms and then looked back at Miss Drake. "You can leave us now, Miss Drake." Lenore waved her away. "I am done with this costume. It's fine as it is. I won't have you fussing over it all day. My companion and I have things to plan."

Her smile was glowing as she stared at me. I thought sure Miss Drake could hear the beating of my heart. I doubted that old, dark woman could understand anything of passionate love. She was up to no good and I did not trust her in the least. Each time I spied her, I could not help but think of that cup I left with Victoria.

I watched as Miss Drake, lips pursed, removed the lovely medieval dress from over Lenore's head and walked briskly past me and out the door without saying another word.

Lenore stood in the middle of the room in her petticoat. It was all I could manage to stop myself from running to her and helping her out of it completely. She sighed, a look of disgust on her face.

"I so wish this ball was a thing of the past. I am weary of everyone's fuss over it." She paused and her eyes lit up as she looked at me. "I have a surprise for you. I've convinced Mama that you shall attend the ball as an invited guest of Foster and me."

I was shocked and surprised.

"Well, I own that I should love to be present, of course..." I paused as I heard my words stammer out. "I so love to dance." It was true. Dancing was something I enjoyed greatly when my family hosted dinner parties and balls. But that all seemed so far away now.

Lenore moved in closer. I could feel the heat from her body.

"We won't be able to dance together, my dear Annalee, but at least we will be with each other at the ball."

Her eyes searched mine for some sense of acceptance. She knew she could offer nothing more. And I knew it too. Would that ever be enough? Admiring the woman I loved from the far side of a room at a ball?

"Please say you will, darling Annalee."

As if I could deny you anything?

I smiled as wide as I could. "I am behaving like a ninny," I said. "Of course I shall be honored to be a guest and be with you. I was just so amazed at the invitation."

"Then you shall come," Lenore said, the delight evident. But she suddenly grew serious. "Oh, but what shall you wear? I'm certain Foster and Miss Drake only brought costumes for him and for me..."

"I have something special I can wear," I said in a low voice. Lenore had no way of knowing what I had brought with me in my luggage. At the bottom of my large travel bag, wrapped in an old sheet, I kept the only thing I did not allow the creditors to take from me. My mother's wedding dress--the stiff ivory satin bead and overdress of Brussels lace looped up over the satin with lovely knots of orange blossom. For some reason, it was the one thing of my mother's that I clutched and would not let go. I suppose at the time, it was the most cherished reminder of the woman I loved so dearly and I barely got to know.

She would want me to wear it now.

"Oh, how wonderful, Annalee. I'm certain we can find or make a masquerade mask for you."

She stood too close for my lack of control. Her eyes said she wanted me and I very much wished to comply, but now that Lord Blackstone and Miss Drake were back, Lenore was no longer mine. I had to leave before I got both Lenore and myself in trouble. I smiled, feinting excitement.

"Pick a mask for me, Lenore. I will love it."

I had to leave. The scent of her skin, the glow of her golden hair and soft, moist lips that beckoned was too much to bear. I walked out, the pain in my heart at parting like a knife forever planted there.

It was settled. I, Annalee Stewart, would attend the Masquerade Ball and not dance with the Lady Blackstone, the woman I loved fiercely, the woman I had perhaps foolishly given my heart to.

It was with such heavy heart that I left, that I had completely forgotten to ask Lenore if she had stopped drinking the chocolate.

Twenty Four

The two days that passed before the Ball were spent mostly making sure Cyrano had his daily walks. I hardly saw Lenore, and always with Miss Drake hovering over her. I tried to be inconspicuous as I looked around her sitting room for any sign of a cup with chocolate, but did not see it. Was she drinking anything at all? Was Miss Drake taking it away?

Blackstone Castle was alive with extra staff that I had never seen and colorful banners were going up downstairs in the main foyer. Inside, my nerves had my stomach tied up like a knotted rope. I had tried on my mother's dress and was pleasantly relieved to find how well it fit and how beautifully preserved it had remained.

I dressed as the shadowy color of twilight crept into my room leaving the corners in darkness. I lit several candles and finally looked at myself in the mirror. The image reflected there caused a warm and satisfied feeling inside. I had to admit that my looks had never shown better, not even at my coming out ball. Was it the dress, I wondered, and the magic of my mother's love coming through? I had piled my hair into a cascade of golden curls high atop my head. I was frankly amazed that I had done such a fine job on my own hair. It was not something I could master.

The light knock at the door was Betsy.

"Oh, Miss," she breathed in dismay, "You'll be the belle of the ball." Her eyes were wide as she admired every inch of me.

I silently prayed Lenore would look upon me with such attention and adoration.

"You must not exaggerate," I said, smiling. "That position is reserved for Miss Wallis." It was true but it was also a totally foul thought for me.

Betsy shook her head. "She can't hold a candle to you for looks, Miss".

"Dear Betsy, you are prejudiced. And now I'd best go to Lady Blackstone."

As was the norm, I found Miss Drake with Lenore. Lenore looked resplendent in her medieval dress and pale gold curls fashioned after the hair styles of the day. Miss Drake's sharp gaze took in every detail of my dress when I walked into the room.

Lenore let out a low gasp and her eyes opened wide in surprise. Miss Drake shot a disapproving stare at her but Lenore reacted by dismissing her.

"Thank you, Miss Drake. We're done here. That will be all."

I never saw that woman move so fast. I was so proud of my Lenore that I wished to hug her hard.

"Oh Annalee, you look so beautiful." She rushed to me, standing inches away, admiring me with a look of wonder in her eyes. "In that gown you resemble a glowing moonbeam."

"That's so poetic," I replied, so wanting to just forget all these fancy dresses and the Ball and just make love to my Lenore.

"You inspire me to poetry, my Annalee."

I looked at her, consumed with love. It was she who was truly aglow tonight. But her hair did not do her justice. Miss Drake had not done Lenore proper. Not for tonight. My darling had to outshine everything, including that wicked Miss Clarisse Wallis.

"Lenore, will you allow me to loosen your hair the merest trifle? Miss Drake arranged it a bit stiffly I'm afraid."

I let down some of her longer hair and allowed the ringlets to fall around her face. Now she looked like the goddess she was. A shame she had to hide her beauty behind a mask tonight.

She looked in the mirror and clapped her happy approval. "How clever you are, my Annalee." Reaching out, she took both my hands and pulled me away. "Now come, grab the two masks on the chair and we must go down, for the Wallises will be arriving at any moment."

And again, I wanted to ask about the chocolate but she whisked me away and out the door but suddenly stopped, causing me to nearly run into her.

"Quick, put your mask on," she said, handing me the stunning mask with massive and colorful bird feathers. But it was her mask that was breathtaking, covered in sequins and jewels with sweeping wings extending beyond her head.

We tied each other's masks and quickly hurried downstairs.

We'd barely reached the main hall when the butler announced the Wallises. Clarisse Wallis swept in on her father's arm. She came regaled in an Elizabethan dress, replete with large, stiff collar and pearls woven through her piled hair. I grudgingly had to admit that she did look magnificent, but not as magnificent as the woman by my side. Sadly, I suddenly realized how insignificant I truly was.

Other guests began to arrive in earnest and Lenore, with a little smile, left my side and went to stand beside the Earl in greeting the guests. The main castle hall quickly filled with couples resplendent in period costumes and elegant masks. I wondered where the Dowager could be. And Victoria? Would she be here? Would she have any information?

Two butlers that I did not recognize began to usher us toward what I assumed was the Blackstone Castle Grand Ballroom. A room I still had not been privy to visiting.

What kind of night would this be? I knew I had to stay close to Lenore and hoped the Earl spent most of his time soliciting the adoring overtures of Miss Wallis rather than beside his wife.

Twenty Five

The Grand Ballroom of Blackstone Castle took my breath away. Literally. I had to remember to close my mouth as I walked in with the others into a room I fashioned only the best theaters in London could rival.

Towering stone columns rose from the floor to the high ceiling on both sides. Candles burned on every table that lined the length of the right side, while muted colored stain-glass windows glittered to my left, which opened to a terrace outside. Banners and flags hanging from the ceiling floated as a slight breeze played gently from the opened windows. Food and goblets of drink covered the tables. At the far end of the ballroom, directly opposite the double doors we'd come through, stood a raised platform with a band of musicians.

I stared with amazement around me at all the guests with their costumes and wild masks and wondered if this is what such a night might have looked like centuries ago.

It certainly was magical and I was lost in all its glory; so lost that I momentarily lost sight of Lenore and the Earl. I finally spotted them, Miss Wallis and another gentleman I did not recognize because of the full mask he wore, in the center of the room. Everyone had parted into groups on either side, allowing for them to be the focus. I still searched for a dark corner where I could become as a fly on the wall and observe.

The music began and the Earl opened the Ball with Miss Wallis and Lenore with the heretofore unknown dance companion. As they swirled about the dance floor, other couples joined in. I wanted to shrink further back into the wall I had selected for myself when a voice from behind startled me.

"The companion's fate again, Miss Stewart?"

I turned around to see a figure in scarlet velvet doublet and pants, a large, floppy hat and sporting a satin mask with gold lace and plumage. The mask did not cover the gentleman's entire face. Did I know this man? The eyes....

Before I could even respond, he wrapped a strong arm around my waist and pulled me to the dance floor. I wasn't frightened, but who could this insolent gentleman be? I considered pasting a nice slap to his face when the dance concluded but as he lifted the floppy brim of the scarlet hat, the blazing green eyes behind the mask were unmistakable.

"Will you give me the pleasure of this dance, Annalee Stewart?"

How could I pull away now and leave Victoria standing in the middle of the ballroom? Why was she dressed as a male courtier from Henry the Eighth's court? Had the Dowager allowed her daughter to costume herself as a man in public or had Victoria sneaked in? No one could guess it was a woman in this costume, let alone that it was the sister of the Earl.

She held me in strong, firm arms as we danced and it was near impossible to control my curiosity regarding the cup I'd left with her. But we were dancing very tightly knit and a conversation could easily be overheard. I inhaled a subtle scent of clove and cinnamon on her clothes. It was a heady, arousing combination. I was suddenly overwhelmed with the desire to sink my face into her shoulder and linger there to catch more of the fragrance.

We continued to dance, while I tried valiantly not to let my eyes stray too often to the crowd in search of Lenore and her mysterious dancing partner. When the music finally stopped, Victoria did not immediately release me. She gazed down intently at me.

"Tomorrow, down by Blackheart River, at strike of noon. Meet me." Her voice was a low whisper.

I inhaled in surprise and excitement. She had news! I nodded inconspicuously. Victoria smiled wide, bowed and kissed my hand. My cheeks must have shone much like the red glowing lamps upon a fancy carriage and there was a tingly, giggly fluttering in my belly.

"I'll bring you something refreshing and then we must part, I fear, for my mother does not know where I am or who I am and if she finds me, I'm afraid I won't be a very presentable dance partner for Mr. Birnbaum, the young, who seems to be doing quite well with Lenore."

She was gone as I stood trying to understand why my insides fluttered like a flock of birds in flight each time this woman was near me. The reaction disturbed me. It set my stable emotions off balance. I had given my heart to

Lenore. Had Victoria Blackstone stolen a small piece for her own?

I shook my head to clear my thoughts and searched around the room for Lenore. I had to fill my sight with every inch of her.

"Here is a glass of ratafia, my dear Lady." Victoria leaned in close and whispered. "Until tomorrow, dear Annalee." She bowed, handed me the small glass of the drink and disappeared into the crowd of costumed guests.

Left a bit flustered and confused, I looked around once more for my Lenore, but was suddenly distracted by Miss Wallis's voice. She laughed loud enough for me to hear it from across the room, and then I noticed many of the couples and guests began strolling out onto the terrace through the open windows.

Trying to remain as inconspicuous as I could, I made my way toward the terrace and soon spotted Lenore, who appeared to be with the Dowager, who wore no mask but heavily white powdered face, large painted beauty mark and a wig of piled high white hair.

Marie Antoinette she wished! I chuckled heartily inside.

I picked up my stride to meet up with them. My heart beat stronger as Lenore's eyes sparkled at the sight of me and she smiled warmly. I wanted to take her in my arms and smother her with hungry kisses.

"Oh, Miss Stewart, are you enjoying the ball? Have you danced? I own, I feel somewhat fatigued already. Have you seen Foster?"

Why would she care where her husband was?

"The Dowager is in search of him, you see," she added swiftly, almost realizing my inner thoughts.

"I saw the Earl dancing with Miss Wallis," I said, not caring one bit where they might be.

"There they are now," the Dowager said.

The two were walking up the steps at the end of the terrace.

"What a charming effect the moonlight gives to the park below." Miss Wallis was talking in a loud voice. Had she had too much to drink? She suddenly turned and looked directly at Lenore. "Come, Lady Blackstone, I am quite sure one can see for miles tonight. Think of the panorama to be observed from the upper battlements." She turned to the Earl, who stood with a smug smile and acting as if his wife did not exist. "Can we not go up and see the view by moonlight? I should like it of all things." The vixen smiled coyly at him.

"Certainly, if you wish it," he said agreeably.

No, of course, he would refuse her nothing.

Miss Wallis clapped her hands in delight, the little minx that she was. She looked back at Lenore.

"You must come too, Lenore, and the Dowager too."

I knew I didn't count as a human being in her eyes, so no, I was not insulted to be excluded from the invitation. But I'd be damned if I was going to let Lenore go up to those battlements feeling fatigued without me.

Several people in the terrace came up to inquire what was afoot.

"We are to have a conducted tour of the battlements by moonlight," cried Miss Wallis, and sped to the narrow stairs while a large throng of guests followed her. They surged up the narrow stairway, Lenore being swept along with them. I struggled against some of the crowd, attempting to keep up with Lenore who seemed alarmed.

Miss Wallis seized Lenore's hand and pulled her toward the parapet.

"Do but look down, Lenore. Is it not a magnificent night? Let's stand on this stone slab in order to see better."

They were too close to the edge. I pushed and shoved and reached them. I saw Lenore follow Miss Wallis's pointing hand below, but Lenore flinched and closed her eyes instead.

Suddenly, another party of people reached the top of the stairway, pressing those of us already there forward. Lenore was thrust against the parapet. She screamed wildly and swayed. She was going over! I pushed one woman to the floor and maneuvered past her just in time to clutch a fold of Lenore's dress, grabbing one of her hands. I hung on to her. If my love was going over the side of the castle, I was going with her.

Soon, others were reaching out and supporting Lenore and drawing her back. She looked at me with the eyes of a wild, frightened animal.

"Someone pushed me!" She fell back, fainting, into my arms.

Twenty Six

Everything after that seemed to move as in a blur, the Earl rushing Lenore from my arms and carrying her away, and screaming for everyone to stay back.

I saw that Miss Wallis followed, so I decided I also had a rightful place by Lenore's side in the eyes of all present.

The Earl took Lenore to her bedroom, laid her down gently and chafed her delicate hands to his.

"I would not have had such a thing happen for all the world," bemoaned Miss Wallis. "I had not a notion that Lenore was in a nervous state or I would not have suggested going up to the battlements. I blame myself."

Vain woman that she was, she never stopped craving attention to herself. And her lamentations were quite questionable. I didn't like the look of complacency Lord Blackstone gave her.

"There is no real damage done," he said, still holding Lenore's hand. "See, she is coming around already."

Lenore's eyelids fluttered and she stared up at the worried faces bent over her. Her gaze stopped at Miss Wallis and she shuddered violently.

"You are quite safe, my dearest," said the Earl softly. "Why not lay back and rest."

"Someone pushed me," whispered Lenore. "I felt someone push me. How can I forget that?"

I rather enjoyed the flash of anger in my love's eyes. Had someone pushed her? But who and for what ungodly reason?

"There were certainly a great many guests pressing around," insisted the Earl soothingly, "and you were standing in an elevated position after all. Someone, anyone could have bumped into you, certainly, but not on purpose, Lenore." He patted her hand. "Try not to think of it, dear, and rest."

He turned to look at Miss Wallis. "Miss Wallis, you must return to the ball or your guests will be wondering what has happened to you."

"You must go back with her, Foster," murmured Lenore. "I wish for Miss Stewart to remain however."

Lord Blackstone looked at me with an uncertain gaze. He didn't trust me. I could see it on his face.

"I prefer to have Miss Drake come and look after you, Lenore. She can be of more help than Miss Stewart." He eyed me under dark, suspicious eyebrows. "Nothing against you, of course, Miss Stewart. You are welcome to join the ball with Miss Wallis and I."

He kissed Lenore on the forehead and walked out with Miss Wallis. Lenore had closed her eyes again, distressing me to no end. I worried what kind of setback this would have on her. And now I had to relinquish control of her to a woman I suspected harbored ill intent toward my Lenore.

I had no choice but to follow the Earl and Miss Wallis from the room. But I could not, would not, leave my love and pretend to have a great time at a ball I had no interest in. I stopped when we reached the door to exit the sitting room.

"I shall remain here in the sitting room, Lord Blackstone, if you don't mind, in case the Lady should have need of me."

"Very well, Miss Stewart," he sighed, more interested now in getting away than in stopping me from staying. He and Miss Wallis, her arm circled around his, left in haste.

I sat down in Lenore's favorite chair with troubled mind. Could it be that someone had attempted to push her over the parapet or was it merely fancy engendered by her fear of heights? It was certainly true that the swell of people up the narrow stairway could have given Lenore a false impression of being purposely pushed. Still, I believed her.

The door to Lenore's room opened and Miss Drake approached me. She stood there with her grey demeanor and odd smirk on her face.

"There is no call for you to wait here, Miss," she said, half insolently. "Doctor Llewellyn will be here shortly and once he administers the draught, Lady Blackstone won't wake till the morning."

I had no recourse but to go to my room, tears of frustration my only consolation.

The following morning I awoke with a foggy brain and still in my mother's dress. The mask lay on the floor and for the first time, I noticed small tears in the fabric. I nearly wept, for the dress was my most cherished possession and the only piece I had left of my mother on this earth.

But I must have slept too late, for I did not feel rested. How I could have slept at all was beyond me so sick from worry was I over what happened last night. All I knew was that I had to get to Lenore. And then there was Victoria. We were to meet today by Blackheart River.

I removed the dress as gingerly as I could, making sure not to cause further damage, and laid it out on my bed. It would have to wait. I had no idea what time it was since I had no timepiece in my room but no one had been to my door knocking for breakfast. What time could it be?

I hurriedly splashed some water from the basin, dressed in my grey day dress, wrapped a shawl around my shoulders, arranged my mussed hair as best I could and tied the bonnet under my chin.

There was no leaving the castle before I checked on Lenore. My stomach felt empty and tight. I was hungry but knew I could not eat a bite.

Just as I went to knock on her door, it suddenly opened and a short, wiry-haired man holding a large black bag stood before me. Behind him stood the stone-faced Miss Drake.

"Pardon me, sir, I meant no disrespect," I said. "I was going to merely knock and inquire over Lady Blackstone's health. I'm her companion, you see."

He cleared his throat after looking me over carefully.

"Ahh," he said, glancing back at Miss Drake. "Well, there is no cause for anxiety, I believe," he said judiciously.

"With rest and proper care, Lady Blackstone should eventually be restored to health again."

I took a deep breath and voiced my question.

"Do you suggest a change of scenery might not do the Lady good, Doctor Llewellyn? A trip away from the castle might improve her spirits?"

I heard Miss Drake inhale in shock. But the doctor nodded, deep thought lines etched on his old face.

"Yes, yes, I do believe it would do her very well to take a trip, young lady." He looked at Miss Drake, who eyed me with venom. "See if the Earl can't arrange a nice get away for he and Lady Blackstone. Perhaps a cottage in the countryside. Somewhere quiet and restorative."

Lenore would be going far, far away with me, that was certain.

The doctor left and Miss Drake gleefully informed me that Lenore was asleep and promptly closed the door in my face.

I rushed down the main stairs and saw that the time in the large clock in the hall was just seconds before marking the noon hour. Picking up my skirts, I ran out the door just as the loud tones began to echo through Blackstone.

Twenty Seven

The day was dark. And windy. I had to fasten my bonnet tighter as it was nearly swept from my head as I sped down the path to the river's edge below. And I had to hold down my shawl for fear that would blow right off my shoulders.

Victoria Blackstone waited for me near the old tower. She stood by her large horse, a tall, lean cloaked figure, dark against the grey of the land. The river gurgled by in a strong current.

She watched me approach, her features drawn and as mirthless as the color of the bleak clouds circling above us. But her green eyes greeted me with a smile and I returned her warm gaze with one of my own.

"I was afraid I'd miss you," I said, trying to catch my breath from running so far. "After last night, I managed to oversleep, although I feel as I hadn't slept in days."

She looked away, and I suddenly felt robbed of that emerald gaze.

"I learned about it and saw the commotion in the ballroom, but wasn't anywhere near to be of any help." She paused and moved closer, searching my face intently. "I'm glad you came to me with your suspicions, Annalee."

Victoria pulled Lenore's cup from beneath her cloak and looked at it with loathing. "There is more than just a trace of belladonna in that cup. Enough to cause great harm to any living thing that drank of it." The wind whipped wisps of her wine-hued hair about her face and she grew silent, jaw firmly set.

Everything seemed to stop moving around me. The wind stilled, the waters of Blackheart River grew silent. My heart was the only thing I heard banging in my ears.

"Annalee?" Victoria's voice broke the trance. "You were right," she said, staring at me with one brow raised. "Did you hear me?"

"You are certain?" I fumbled the question, barely able to speak.

"I trust the woman who tested the remains of the chocolate in the cup, if that is what you mean. If Miss Drake has been insisting Lenore drink this poisonous concoction, as you say, then by God, there is all reason to suspect there is foul play involved."

My mind was still racing to make connections. Belladonna. I didn't know that much about plants or gardening or herbs but I knew belladonna was a commonly used and potent poison. But why would Miss Drake want to poison Lenore? And did it have any connection to the conversation I overheard between she and the Earl? I nearly choked on the thought. Was the Earl involved? No, it was too evil to even contemplate.

Victoria took hold of both my arms and looked at me with fiery determination in her eyes.

"Annalee, we must proceed carefully. Confronting Miss Drake or telling my brother or Lenore won't help. Lenore must not drink anymore of that poisoned chocolate. You must make sure of that. I'm afraid that the poison might already be too far into her system. You must make sure she gets up and about. Get her outside into the sun. Take walks with Cyrano."

"But what shall we do about Miss Drake?" I said quietly, for once overwhelmed by the evil facing us. "Should she not be kept away from Lenore?"

Unexpectedly, the woman before me smiled wistfully, sadness creeping into her usually amused eyes.

"You've done so much for Lenore. Her health improved because of you, you must know. You have my undying thanks for that."

A dark cloud drifted overhead, casting her face in shadows. Her gaze moved away from me, toward the dense forest across the river.

"Lenore's decline began during the first months of her marriage, a marriage which should never have taken place. It was loveless and with the miscarriage and no hope of a child, it was a burden too heavy for her heart. It was all so wrong," Victoria said, her mood suddenly violent. "She was like a windflower then, and now—"

She suddenly squared her shoulders and looked at me with a tear rolling down her cheeks.

"I beg your pardon, Annalee. I am embarrassing you. I should not have spoken in that fashion."

It was then that I knew. I knew what Lenore meant to Victoria Blackstone.

"You're in love with her," I said, trying to swallow the lump in my throat.

She smiled sadly. "I was, yes, at one time. But it was ill-fated to be unrequited for all eternity. She was my brother's bride."

Victoria reached out, took my chin and tipped it up towards her, forcing my eyes to focus on hers.

"And once again, my heart has taken the path to heartbreak and rejection. Have I even a chance, a hope for a small space in your heart, my dearest Annalee?"

I could not respond. The words did not form upon my lips. Victoria Blackstone was professing love, out here in the middle of a flowing river and towering cliff, causing my heart and my head to spin out of control.

Her penetrating eyes held mine for a few seconds longer, then looked away as she sighed. Her body stiffened and her voice was low when she looked back at me.

"You, my dearest Annalee, have loved Lenore from the first. And I was not blind to how she took to you." She paused, not taking her gaze from me. "You have made love to Lenore. You need not answer, I know it to be true. Only someone intimately and passionately in love would have dared take such a risk as you did by bringing me this cup and voicing your suspicions."

Should I run away now? How much could my heart bear?

"The only thing we share is Lenore. We must proceed with care, as I said." She put the cup back inside her cloak. "I shall take this as evidence and will hide it in my room safe from the prying and curious eyes of my mother and nosy servants. Meanwhile, please try to never leave Lenore's side and make certain she takes no more of that drink. The both of us must keep our eyes and ears open and alert. Do not hesitate to come in search of me if you see or hear anything I should know about."

She suddenly took me in her arms and kissed me; a very gentle, delicate kiss tasting of cinnamon. I should have pulled away. But God help me I did not want to. My heart belonged to Lenore, but I did not desire to escape from Victoria's strong arms and my mouth remained wanting more.

I closed my eyes as she pulled away, holding back the tears that I felt were ready to burst forth.

"Victoria, I—"

"Please, don't," she smiled. "Let us save Lenore from those who wish her harm and leave all else to fate."

She withdrew from me and immediately I felt a cold wind take her place. Dear Lord, I wanted her to stay. I wanted her embrace. My thoughts jumbled and heart torn, I watched her ride away, the horse kicking up moist clumps of sand behind it.

I walked slowly back up the river bank and toward the path up the hill. I paid no mind to the wind which had intensified and shrieked around me in mournful song. No, the thoughts going through my mind were as furious as any wind could be. Someone was trying to kill Lenore and somehow, my heart had been torn asunder by two women.

Twenty Eight

My heart remained restless all day. I went often to inquire over Lenore but each time was rebuffed by Miss Drake. I was so desperate to see Lenore, to gaze into her eyes, to be certain she was safe. A growing fear that she might be in danger for her life threatened to overwhelm me and send me off to Victoria. Had she not insisted I remain with Lenore at all times? I knew not what that witch Drake was feeding Lenore, if anything at all.

I burst into tears locked in my room until I finally decided it would do me no good to just cry. It was time to walk Cyrano. It was also a good excuse to worm my way into Lenore's room where Cyrano was.

Alas, I found out that the Earl had ordered Cyrano removed to the downstairs servants' quarters so that Lenore could get complete rest. Lord help me, my love was totally in the hands of those who would do her harm!

I resolved that if I could not see Lenore come tomorrow, I would force my way in. But that would no doubt lead to my immediate dismissal and possibly seal the fate of the woman I loved. No. A better plan was to go to Victoria. Victoria. I shook the memory of her arms wrapped around me and her mouth, so warm on mine. How had this woman suddenly become my last hope?

After a very lonely dinner in my room which I barely nibbled at, I decided I simply had to do something, anything to keep my frustration from exploding into all out panic.

I collected Cyrano from Betsy and strolled through the courtyard and out into the park with him. The strong wind from earlier had calmed down to barely a whisper. It was dusk but not yet dark and the warmth of the earth drew out the light perfume of the flowers around me.

For Cyrano, he seemed to be enjoying the many delights of the evening, but suddenly, something spooked him and he darted away wildly racing ahead of me toward the cliff path down to the river. I had no desire to lose him, let alone have him go down to the river and into the water. Not when it was already approaching a deepening evening sky.

Lifting my skirts to move without tripping, I ran quickly after him, calling to him by name, but without results. He was halfway down the path and down to Blackheart River. I called again.

"Cyrano!" But he kept running. What was down there?

The waters of the river were merely a low lullaby but the woods across the way were inky dark and the tall trees swayed to the very light wind. I wanted to find Cyrano and get back to the castle before the sky turned black.

I found him sniffing behind one of the craggy rocks that clustered near the cliff side. Now was my chance to grab him before he could take off again.

"You, bad boy," I said aloud. "No more walks for you tonight." I gathered him up in my arms and held on tight.

As I looked across the river, I paused. There was someone rowing from the woods toward the river bank. The boat looked familiar. I looked toward the tower where a small boat always bobbled and it was gone. Who had taken the boat and crossed into the dense forest? And for what purpose?

Against my better judgment, I decided to conceal myself behind the rocks, hugging the little dog to me even tighter. I couldn't have him barking and give me away.

It was a man in the boat, and I watched as he approached the tower, rowed to shore, and secured the skiff once again. I had to get closer. I was already committed, regardless of the obvious danger I could be getting myself into.

Crouching and moving quietly, Cyrano securely clutched to my chest, I moved to a closer set of rocks further down the path and very near the tower. The man held a clump of plants in his hands. For some reason, I thought I had seen him before. The last glimmer of sun was disappearing fast, but I suddenly realized who he was. It was one of the grooms at the castle! What could he be doing out here?

I watched as he paused and looked about cautiously, until finally knocking on the old door of the tower. To my utter shock, the door creaked open, and there in the doorway stood Miss Drake! She motioned the groom to come inside after peeking around him, then closed the door shut.

For a moment, I was unable to move, but curiosity compelled me to go further. I needed to know more. Perhaps I could overhear what they were saying inside.

There was only a narrow stream of water that split from the river and separated the tower from the bank, so I silently prayed Cyrano would remain quiet and still. I waded into the running stream and into the ankle deep water. I made sure to not splash as I moved.

There was a tiny window in the crude rock tower that had been covered with a piece of sacking. But one corner was folded back and through the gap, I could see Miss Drake and the groom talking together. He had handed her the plants, for she held them in her hands. Belladonna? My body tensed. The rush of water felt cool on my legs. How would I explain my very wet dress and feet when I returned to the castle?

The two appeared to be arguing but to my disappointment, with the sound of the flowing river, I could not distinguish what they said. Cyrano squirmed restlessly in my arms. I suppose he grew tired of a hand over his muzzle. Still, I could not risk him prying free from me and taking off or barking.

I reluctantly and cautiously backed away, being careful not to fall in the water. It was impossible to hear what that horrible woman and the groom were saying so there was very little to be gained by staying and much danger in remaining. The man could come out of the tower at any moment and catch me spying.

Once I was a good distance from the tower, I glanced back once to make sure no one had opened the door and seen me. I hurried up the cliff path, suddenly overwhelmed by a nameless dread. I was gripped with a feeling that a miasma of evil hovered over Blackstone

Castle, with Miss Drake as its arch priestess and Lenore as its focal point.

Try as I might to persuade myself that I was being extreme and dramatic, I could not squelch the fears. Miss Drake was putting poison in Lenore's drink. She wanted to murder her. Someone had pushed Lenore, possibly hoping to accomplish the same thing. And what business was Miss Drake up to with one of the castle's grooms in a tower that all thought abandoned, even Victoria? Was the groom gathering the poisonous plants for her? And did Lord Blackstone know?

I shivered violently at this last thought. Lenore lay in her own bedroom and under Drake's power. I was not able to get to her.

Heaven help me. What should I do? What could I do?

Twenty Nine

My stomach nervous and upset, I barely touched the beef brisket and corn brought to my room. I'd been able to sneak back without anyone seeing my soaked dress. After supper, I tried one more time to see Lenore and was again met with the sour countenance of Miss Drake. Lenore, she said, was getting better but still needed complete rest.

If I did not see Lenore tomorrow morning, I would find the Earl and offer a formal complaint. I had to cloak my inquiry with professional interest. Had I not been hired to do a job as companion to Lady Blackstone? Would I not be able to do that which was required of me? I wasn't at all certain going to the Earl was the most proper thing, but if that didn't work, Victoria had to know that I was being purposely kept away from seeing Lenore and that I feared for her life.

I spent a wakeful night, tossing and turning and finding no peace in the quiet and dark of the early morning hours. My thoughts and apprehensions were like harpies, picking at my brain, leaving only the worst of my imaginings. The lone candle was burning down to just a flicker.

The sense of dread, of something evil breathing down the neck of my beloved Lenore was palpable. I thought I would go mad if I did not see her. I had to know if she was awake and improving as I'd been told.

I knew I had to tell Victoria what I had seen at the tower. I remembered what she had said. We were to be sure of every step we took. Accusing Miss Drake without concrete evidence could prove risky. We had to catch her in the act. Suppose Victoria and I went to Miss Drake with my tale? She could deny it and who could prove she was lying and not me?

Unable to sleep, I got up and decided to splash some water on my face to keep me awake for the remainder of the night. I knew I would get no sleep. That was when I heard it.

It was a loud cry from outside in the hallway! A woman's voice.

Dear God, Lenore!

My face still wet and my dress barely fastened, I grabbed the candle and ran down the darkened hallway. There was only silence. Then I heard it again. It was Lenore. I ran, my heart beating so hard I thought it would burst forth from my chest in flight. I didn't knock, just shoved the door open, not caring if I found Drake there. Not caring about anything but Lenore.

The sitting room was pitch-dark with not a candle lit. How fortunate that I had brought mine, nearly exhausted as it was. The drapes were completely drawn.

"Lenore," I called.

Again, I heard a low moan come from her bedroom. My eyes adjusted and I noticed the door to her bedroom was open and candlelight glimmered from the crack of the open door.

I ran, stumbling on the rug, into her room, fully expecting to fight off Miss Drake. But there was no sign of the wicked woman, only a room dark with death.

Lenore lay barely moving in her bed, hair loose and matted, a white nightgown loosely hanging on her dreadfully thin frame. It was as if she had withered away these few days.

I rushed to her side, throwing myself beside her on the bed. She uttered another cry of discomfort, placing a bone-thin hand to her stomach.

"My dear God, what have they done to you, my darling Lenore?" I cried in pain as I brushed away some of her now faded hair from her face. She was so cold to the touch and her lips had lost all their color.

When she looked at me, the blue of her eyes had dimmed and the sparkle gone.

"Annalee." Her voice was only a weak whisper. "It hurts." She put her hand to her stomach again. It was the poison. I knew it.

I looked desperately around for any sign of cups and although it was dark in the room with one candle burning, I saw one cup sitting on the small table by her bedside. There was a puddle of chocolate at the bottom. I controlled the fury and pain that split my heart asunder. I was too late.

My stomach lurched and I had to fight down the bile threatening in my throat. I leaned my head back, fighting away the tears coming down my cheeks.

"Oh my darling Lenore, have you been taking the chocolate that woman as forced upon you?"

I knew she had. I knew it because my Lenore was dying. I could do nothing anymore to save her. It was all too late. But I still had to fight for what life she had left.

"Come Lenore, you must sit up. Come, sit up and let me read you something..."

She put her hand over mine to still me.

"I cannot sit up, my Annalee. I...it hurts." She grimaced in discomfort.

"I shall go for the Earl." I panicked. I didn't know what to do or say.

"No, stay with me, Annalee. You said you would never leave." What was left of life in her eyes pleaded with me.

"You cannot leave me, Lenore. I live for you. We are going away together, remember? Do not leave me." I cried openly as I held her waif-like body and stroked her long hair.

"We loved, Annalee," she whispered in my ear, her breath stale of poison. "Always remember that. I never thought I would be loved as you loved me."

I shook my head violently.

"Memories are nothing but cruel torment. They bring yearnings for times, people, things you shall never have again." I was bitter and it was an empty life Lenore was bequeathing me. "I could not bear to live without you," I said, wiping the wetness from my face.

I cradled her, burying my head on her chest. But Lenore had gone still and so had her heart. So quiet. I looked at her and knew she was gone. Her eyes had closed in peace, face serene.

"No," I wailed, not caring who heard me. I laid her gently back on the bed and felt a raging fire from within and the room closed in on me. I feared I would faint but I didn't. Instead, I reached for the cup on the table and ran, ran as if the hounds of hell were at my heels ready to tear me to shreds.

Thirty

I ran with a fevered mind and shattered heart. I didn't remember how long it took me to get to the door of the Dower House or how I had made it through the pitch dark woods, but there I stood, banging loudly at this ungodly hour of the morning at the house of the Dowager. I wasn't thinking clearly or logically. I was only thinking of Victoria. She had to know. She had to come.

I knocked harder and longer at the door until a sleepy-eyed butler opened the door, candle in hand.

"I must see Victoria Blackstone. She will see me, Annalee Stewart. Please hurry and fetch her."

He stared at me, his grey mustache droopy; his eyes still struggled to remain open. And he barred my way. I shoved him to the side and barged into the darkened foyer hall.

"Miss," he protested, "Miss, you must not come any further."

I turned, my anger ready to erupt. It would not be a pretty sight if that happened.

"Please inform Miss Blackstone that Annalee is here. Something has happened at the Blackstone Castle."

The foolish man just moved slowly toward the steps of the staircase, staring at me. It was obvious he was deathly afraid of me. No doubt, I was easy to mistake for a mad woman.

From the top of the huge, sweeping stairs, the Dowager stood, holding a large candle, her sleep cap dislodged and side ways, her long gown aglow in candlelight.

"What is the meaning of this, Miss Stewart? Have you gone mad? Are you with drink? What could you want with my daughter at this hour? Has something gone wrong at Blackstone Castle?"

"Annalee, what is wrong?"

Victoria was rushing past her mother and down the stairs tucking a puffy sleeved shirt into black pantaloons. She came and took both my arms.

"Tell me, are you alright?" Her green eyes were wide with alarm. Then she saw the cup I still clutched in my hand. "Lenore?"

Again, the tears poured down my face.

"She is gone. They've murdered her."

"What is this deranged young lady babbling about, Victoria?" The Dowager was slowly making her way down the stairs.

Victoria grabbed me and pulled me towards the door, taking the cup from my grasp.

"Come, we're leaving. I'll have the stable boy ready my horse. You'll ride with me."

"Victoria, I demand you come back!"

169

All I heard was the Dowager shrieking her daughter's name as Victoria slammed the door shut behind us.

⁓⁓

Blackstone Castle was as dark and silent as I had left it. The candles burning in the hall sconces were down to nearly nothing.

Victoria, holding a lantern she'd grabbed from the Dower House stables, and I ran up the stairs and to Lenore's room in silence. There were no words to be found. We also met no staff or the Earl or the murderous Miss Drake. Where were they?

The door to Lenore's room lay open, exactly as I had left it. Everything in the sitting room remained unchanged. Untouched. No one had been there. I knew because even the rug I had nearly tripped over still lay turned over on its corner.

Victoria stopped, looked back at me and proceeded slowly to Lenore's bedroom. I hesitated. Did I really want to go back in there? I could not bear for my heart to shatter once again at the sight of my Lenore so still and cold.

I was thankful that Victoria understood my emotions. She looked at me in a tender way, a sad smile curled on her lips.

"You don't have to follow me, Annalee. But I must go."

I nodded. "I shall be here waiting. Please forgive me."

She reached out and took my hands, squeezing them gently, then left.

I watched her disappear into the bedroom, feeling the chill gather around me and through me. I hugged myself to suppress the shivers. The image of my lifeless Lenore upon her bed will haunt me for the rest of my life.

Seconds later, Victoria appeared in the doorway and motioned to me with a nod of her head.

"Come in, Annalee. It's okay."

I trusted her. That much was certain or else I would not have sought her out. I had to trust her now.

To my shock and utter horror, Lenore was gone! Her bed was empty. And that wasn't the worst of it. The bed had been neatly made and arranged as if she'd never lain there, dead, only an hour ago.

"This can't be," I said in a whisper. My voice had nearly left me. I looked wildly at Victoria. "Lenore died in my arms right there in that bed. I know because I held her as she breathed her last breath. I swear to you, Victoria, her heart beat no more."

Victoria looked around the room swiftly. "What has happened to Lenore, then? Someone has been here to take her body and then take great care to make it appear that Lenore had not even been in bed. For what purpose and by whom?"

"Miss Drake, that she devil!" I blurted. "It was she who murdered her."

"But Miss Drake alone could not carry a lifeless Lenore alone, all the way down the hall and the stairs."

I suddenly began to suffocate in that room of death. The walls began to close in on me. And then I remembered.

"I know how Miss Drake had help."

Thirty One

On the way down to the river, I told Victoria everything I had seen last night at the tower.

The first glimmer of color and dawn was spreading into the lingering darkness when we reached the tower. The skiff was tethered and bobbed on the river current. The stream of water between the bank and tower had ebbed out and we crossed it, barely getting our feet wet.

Victoria, solemn and quiet since leaving the Dower House, looked at me, her jaw set firm as she grasped the large knob on the door, holding the lantern high.

"I do not have the key to the tower with me since we left in such haste from my house. Pray we won't need it."

The knob turned and with a slight nudge, Victoria was through into the tower. I followed her and to both our amazement, found the tower for all intent and purposes, empty. There were a few old wooden tables, bowls and one broken chair. It smelled damp and there was an odd odor in the dank air.

Victoria picked up one of the bowls and brought to it her nose. She turned it over and showed it to me.

"Slightly damp inside. Someone has used it. For what, we can only guess."

I saw them as the early shafts of sunlight filtered through the opening in the window—footprints.

"Look," I said, pointing to the muddy prints on the rough stone floor.

She eyed them with interest. "Fresh, too."

We both followed the prints to a spot on the stones where they abruptly just vanished.

"There is more than one set of prints," I said.

"At least two," Victoria added. "And they suddenly disappear. That leads me to think..."

She paused, crouched down and began to run her hands over the stone blocks of the floor. She suddenly stopped when she came to a smaller stone that didn't seem to fit the rest of the floor and appeared loose. Victoria pried the stone with her bare fingers and was able to lift the stone away. Inside was a pull rope. She looked at me, a look of stunned surprise on her face.

"Our mystery of the vanishing footprints solved," she said as she yanked the rope.

A solid block of stones lifted up before us slowly with a grinding noise. Darkness gaped below.

"A trap door and a hidden passage," Victoria said, peering deep into the dark below. She held the lantern to illuminate down the narrow stairs. She met my curious and shocked face with a slight smile. "Shall you venture down the passage with me or would you prefer to stay here? It appears quite dry below, but I can guarantee nothing more."

She took a couple of steps down and then held out her hand to me, awaiting my decision. There was no way I was going to stay behind. I would follow Victoria till the end, to wherever it would take us in order to find those who had murdered Lenore.

She'd left the trap door open above, allowing the daylight to filter through and giving us at least some kind of brightness than just a quickly fading lantern to stumble through the darkness. The air was even thicker with moisture down so deep. The steps were hewn of rough stone and we had to tread carefully over the uneven surface.

The passage sloped slightly downwards and I kept as close to the wall as I could. It felt damp to the touch and I could barely see in front of me.

"Where does the air come from," I asked, noting that it wasn't difficult to breathe.

"If this passageway leads to the castle as I suspect, there are several openings by the outer walls," Victoria said, not missing a step. "I always wondered what purpose they served and now I know."

She stopped so suddenly that I ran into her.

"Look, there," she said, pointing to the floor. "Do you see footsteps?" She placed the lantern on the floor to get a better look.

In this gloomy half darkness, how could she see anything? Even with the dim lantern light, it was difficult to discern. I moved closer and peered down at the dirty stone floor. Sure enough, I could make out still muddy foot prints. More than one set.

"They are fairly recent from the looks of them." I looked at her. "Miss Drake and her accomplice?"

Victoria still gazed at the prints. "It's possible. There are three keys to the tower. One is kept by my brother, one by me, and the third hangs in the housekeeper's room. Anyone could obtain the third key if they wanted. It doesn't point irrefutably to Drake."

It was warm in the passage and my patience was wearing thin. Desperation once again threatened to overwhelm me.

"We have all the proof we need to know it was indeed that witch who poisoned Lenore. The cups. You said so yourself."

This time, Victoria reached out and took my shoulder. "We shall have her, my dear Annalee, without a doubt she is guilty of poisoning Lenore. But we must still be slow, precise and sure our evidence leads to her ..." she paused, leaned her head back and wiped the tears in her eyes. "...She will pay. This I swear to you and to Lenore." Victoria smiled slightly. "Let's keep going."

We went only a bit further until the passage ended abruptly and before us was an old, weathered door. There was a rusty bolt in the center. Victoria and I exchanged surprised glances and she used both hands to pry the bolt open. The door slid aside with a creak only to find another, nicer and paneled door barring our progress.

We both spotted the tiny lever tucked away in a recess cut into the stone wall. Without waiting, Victoria pulled the lever and the door swung away slowly and we walked straight into Lenore's bed chambers!

Thirty Two

I stood in stunned silence. The mystery of how Lenore's body could have disappeared without any detection or trace became clear. They took her. They took her body through the hidden passage and Lord knows where they put her. But why?

"All these years being brought up in Blackstone and I never knew of this hidden door or the passage to the tower." Victoria stood in contemplation. "I wonder if my brother knows?" She looked at me. "Not hard to see what happened but why take Lenore away like that? Why not afford proper respects for the dead and her family?"

I bowed my head, the answer too cruel. "The poison. The murdering Miss Drake would not have suspicions arise or examination of Lenore." I felt the room spin.

"Annalee, you do not look well, come into the sitting room."

Victoria wrapped an arm about my waist and led me slowly to Lenore's sitting room. But dear God, Lenore was still there, everywhere. There were memories no matter where I looked. The smell, the visions, Lenore was still alive in this room. I began to suffocate and gasp for air.

Victoria swept me up in her arms and pressed me close to her, holding me tight.

"Annalee, you are as white as a sheet!"

Her face began to fade and the room grew dimmer and dimmer. My legs gave way...

Vague, indistinct light filtered through my eyelids. I opened my eyes to fuzzy and then sharper colors. I was in my room but didn't remember getting there. Of course. I had passed out in Victoria's arms.

I got up slowly, trying to shake the cobwebs from my thoughts. She must have brought me here. We were in Lenore's sitting room after discovering a secret door and passage from Lenore's bedroom to the tower.

But I wore my night shift. Victoria must have undressed me and put me to bed. I felt my cheeks grow hot as the thought of her tucking me in and putting me to bed sent conflicting emotions through me.

I went to the wash basin, splashed some water all over my face and then saw the handwritten note on my dresser beside the basin. The handwriting was exquisite and I noted the signed name: Victoria...

My Dearest Annalee,

Despite giving me quite a scare after fainting last night, I was forced to leave you while you rested. I did make sure you were comfortable in your own bed.

I've gone into Lustleigh with the two cups of poisoned chocolate. I aim to bring the Constable back with me. He will find Drake and any accomplice she might have with her.

I must firmly ask you to not leave your room under any circumstances. Feign illness if you must or find other excuses to remain in your room. Have Betsy bring your food. Do not speak with anyone about Lenore's death, the tower or what we have found. That includes my brother, the Earl.

I insist that you follow my instructions fully for I should be inconsolable if anything were to happen to you, my sweetest Annalee.

All my Love,
Victoria

I read her note one more time. I could understand her concerns but it simply was not logical to lock myself away in my room until she returned. I had to find out what was to happen to me now. Not only had I lost the woman I loved, but who knew what would become of me now. With Lenore's last breath had gone my life, in more ways than one. All that I had worked to accomplish for myself and Lenore, the hard veneer, the portrait of the independent woman, the hard-as-nails survival mode I had built had shattered into a million tiny pieces.

No, I could not stay locked away like a damsel in distress in her tower room. I reached for my grey, worn day dress but found it sullied with mud and grime from the passage and the river sand. My fancy dress would have to do. It was the only one I had left.

Just as I readied my hair, a light knock came outside the door.

"It's Betsy, Miss Stewart."

Betsy! At last I could speak with someone. I thought all in the castle had run off and disappeared. When the maid came in, she cast her gaze to the floor and wore all black instead of her usual. She avoided looking me in the eyes.

"The Earl bade I come and help you with your packing, Miss."

"My packing?" I wasn't really surprised but still shocked at the swift boot in the rear I was being given. The Earl certainly wanted me out of Blackstone Castle in a hurry. I couldn't help but wonder why.

"I won't be needing your help, Betsy, but thank you in any case. I'm quite capable of doing it on my own." And then I thought of the Earl. "Betsy, is the Earl here, at the castle?"

"Yes, Miss, he's downstairs in his library. He's not left it since..." she paused, wringing her hands. "Since the Lady passed."

Betsy was the perfect person to answer my questions without becoming the least suspicious of ulterior motives. She was a naïve and unsullied, sweet girl.

I swallowed hard and asked what I had to know.

"Have arrangements been made for Lady Blackstone?" I had to fight back the tears. "Have funeral plans been announced, I mean? When are her parents and family expected?"

Betsy shook her head slowly. "No, Miss. What I heard tell is that the Lady's remains were sent back to her family in France. That's all we heard downstairs. And with Miss Drake's disappearance, we figured that's what had happened. Maybe she went with the Lady's remains?" Betsy leaned in closer, her face full of concern. "Oh, Miss, please don't let anyone know I mentioned anything to you. I don't want to get in any trouble, you understand. We got enough to handle with one of the groomsmen up and gone too."

Miss Drake gone? I didn't for a minute believe Lenore was sent away to her parents. I couldn't bear to think of what exactly had happened, but she most assuredly was not on her way to France. And now Miss Drake was missing. Was she running away for fear of being arrested for murdering Lenore? And had Miss Drake's accomplice gone off with her or just gone back home to wherever home was?

I looked at Betsy and touched her arm. "I won't say a word to anyone about our conversation and I won't be packing because I'm not leaving. Not yet, anyway. I will speak with the Earl now."

Forgive me, dear Victoria.

Thirty Three

I had no intentions of leaving Blackstone before I found out what happened to Lenore's body and the whereabouts of Miss Drake.

I left Betsy, mouth open, standing in the middle of my room. Praying that Victoria would forgive me for disobeying her wishes, I literally ran down the hall and the stairs and toward the Earl's study near the main sitting room downstairs.

I stood in front of the closed door, took a deep breath of courage and knocked hard.

"Enter," the Earl's voice came from within.

He sat behind a large, mahogany desk embellished with elaborate carvings. The desk was covered with books and papers and a bronze sculpture of a large wolf sat on one end. He wore black, from the black coat, black silk vest and black pantaloons to the black cravat at his neck.

The perfect show for a grieving widower.

I swallowed hard as he eyed me with unwelcome irritation.

"Lord Blackstone, there is something I must say to you."

"Then say it, Miss Stewart," he replied indulgently. "I fully expected you on a coach and off to whatever destination you arranged. With Lenore gone, we no longer have need of your services. And my apologies, but I am not in the habit of providing references." His smile was the picture of arrogance.

It was apparent the man had no conscience and no love for Lenore. I knew I should proceed carefully with the Earl, but I had come to here to have my say.

"It concerns your wife," I said boldly. "I have reason to believe that she was in fact murdered. I know not what has been relayed to you, but she did not die of natural causes."

He got up and stood very still facing me, his gaze piercing.

"What nonsense is this which you speak?" he queried in a low, deep voice. "I trust it is merely that your nerves have got the best of you, Miss Stewart. I should hope you have not become completely deranged."

"No, I am not deranged," I said resolutely, gaining courage. "I have evidence to support the accusations, and they will be furnished to you if you wish it."

"You'd best tell me everything you have, but first, I must know who is concerned in this plot of the murder of my dear wife."

"Miss Drake..." I paused, wondering if I should go any further. "...And I even question Miss Wallis. I really have no proof of Miss Wallis's involvement, but only a strong suspicion. She was standing beside Lady Blackstone when the attempt on her life was made at the parapets. Lady Blackstone was pushed."

There was a look of amazement on the Earl's face. "Miss Wallis? You are completely out of your senses."

"No, Lord Blackstone, I am not. I only ask that you investigate my claims, that is all."

He raised his eyebrows. "And did you not notice that I stood on Lenore's other side, Miss Stewart?"

I thought hard on my recollection of that night. Yes, he was right there standing beside Lenore as well! But could he have done such an evil thing to his own wife? And then the conversation between him and Miss Drake came rushing through my mind like ice water. Could the Earl have been involved in the plotting of his wife's murder?

His eyes narrowed as he studied me closely. "Tell me, since you seem convinced of all your delusions, what makes you believe Miss Wallis involved in such a dastardly plot? What do you divine her motives to be?"

I felt flush. I had hoped he would not pose such questions. However, I was now committed to continue.

"I believe her to be in love with you, to have ambitions to become Lady Blackstone. I have noticed how she looks at you—I am no fool. I have observed her in other ways. She would stop at nothing to achieve her own ends."

The Earl replied calmly. "Well, you are very wholehearted in your dislikes, Miss Stewart. I should not care to be the object of your hatred."

"I do not hate Miss Wallis," I said quickly, "It's Miss Drake that holds that special place in my heart. It was she who carried out the murder of Len...Lady Blackstone."

As soon as the words came forth, I knew I had pushed my luck too far and possibly put myself in an uncomfortable position.

His face grew still and I saw his jaw tighten.

"You haven't a shred of real proof for anything you say. I find you over-zealous and possibly under stress. I think it best you pack and leave at once, Miss Stewart."

"Then you do not think—you do not believe there was a plot to murder your wife?" I stammered, appalled that he simply dismissed me and all I had said without any interest in even checking into it. "And what of Miss Drake? I understand she has vanished. Perhaps she is running away from justice?"

"I do not know Miss Drake's whereabouts. My guess is that since Lenore is gone, she had the common sense and decency to leave, something you seem unable to do."

He moved closer to me. "You have allowed your imagination to run rampant and I must advise you to not speak of this to anyone else. Have you already done so? I sincerely hope you haven't, for I still hold power as your ultimate employer. I have all rights to have you put away where all mad people go to die."

He was right. He could sentence me to eternal confinement where those truly mad are condemned to a slow and torturous death and those not mad are conveniently tucked away for insidious reasons. Even though fear gnawed at my insides, I could not back away now.

I shook my head slowly. There was no way I would reveal to him what Victoria knew and that she was at this moment on her way back here with the law.

Relief poured over his features.

"Then no harm has been done and you are free to travel wherever you must go. But leave now, Miss Stewart." He paused, then suddenly grabbed my arm tightly. Pain shot through me. "If you do not go, who knows if someone might not plot your murder, Miss Stewart." His voice was like velvet darkness. There was evil in his eyes. I tried to pull away, but he held on.

"You are hurting me. I am not well. I must go to my room."

"You will leave Blackstone now!" He screamed.

I twisted my arm around quickly and was able to break away, fleeing like a hare, to the safety of my bed chambers. He had not followed. Thankfully, Betsy was gone and everything was as I left it in my room.

My teeth were chattering. Where was Victoria? What was taking so long? If Victoria did not return by dusk, I planned what my next move would be—what it had to be. I was now fully convinced the Earl could have been accomplice to Lenore's death. With Lenore dead, he had a hassle-free path to wed Clarisse Wallis and make her the new Lady Blackstone and mother to new Blackstone heirs.

Somehow, if Victoria did not return by night, I had to leave Blackstone Castle despite Victoria's note. I had already broken all her commands. But there was no doubt that I had to leave the castle. I knew not where I would go, but I no longer felt safe within these walls.

Thirty Four

I must have fallen into a light sleep for when I woke, dusk had fallen outside. And still no sign of Victoria. Her note still lay on my table. What had happened? Had some trouble befallen her? Was I truly alone in this forsaken place? Fear gathered up in my insides like some malignant growth. I could not bear the thought of losing Victoria at my side. She'd been the strong and loyal presence since my arrival at Blackstone Castle. Why had I not trusted her? Why had I pushed her away?

My choices were not bright. I could not and would not throw myself at the mercy of the Dowager. There was no compassion for me there. I would seek out Betsy or Mrs. Patterson, the housekeeper and cook and hope they would take pity upon me and offer some form of sanctuary until I heard from Victoria

Willing myself to believe that she was delayed for a very good reason and would return for me with reinforcements to seek out and find the murdering Miss Drake, I wrote a quick note to Victoria explaining my actions and where to find me. I left my suitcase and bags, donned my bonnet and shawl, and cautiously unlocked my door. Would the Earl be lurking in the darkened hall? He was the last person I wanted to meet up with.

I carried one candle with me and I raised it to peer out into the corridor. There was no sign of the Earl. There was no one stirring. I had to make my way downstairs to the servants' quarters.

I hurried my steps toward the stairs and had reached the standing when I thought I heard a sound from behind. Just as I turned to check, an explosion of pain went off in the back of my head and someone grabbed me. Everything grew fuzzy and grey...

I opened my eyes only to go into panic. I found myself slung over the Earl's shoulder and I recognized where we were! He was down in the hidden passage.

My head ached vilely and I could not scream for he had stuffed a rough gag into my mouth. It tasted sour. I tried to squirm but both my hands and feet were bound by hard rope that burned into my flesh. He was going to kill me. I knew it.

Dear Lord, how could Victoria find me now?

The Earl carried a lantern in his other hand which he placed on the stone floor when we reached the trap door to the tower. He thrust me violently up onto the dirty floor above, jumped up behind me and secured the trap door as it shut tight.

He was breathing heavily and stopped to wipe the sweat from his face, then looked down at me. He wore the look of evil upon that face.

"Allow me to congratulate you on your perspicacity, Miss Stewart," he said mockingly. "I see you succeeded in dragging my sister into your little conspiracy. I found your note to Victoria and destroyed it. But how disappointing that neither of you found the real mastermind. Miss Wallis is not capable of planning a murder and however much she may have disliked Lenore for having what she very much wanted, she was not involved. Oh, I planned on marrying her as soon as Lenore was out of the way. No, she knows nothing of my scheme. Miss Drake, on the other hand, carried out all my instructions to the last detail. She despised Lenore, but I think you know that. She was a woman with ice in her veins who thought I had an interest in her, the old hag..." He laughed. "She did indeed poison my wife at my command. And just like Lenore, she served her purpose and I paid her..." He smiled wide. "No one will ever find where I put her body. But you were wrong about one thing, Miss Stewart. You see, I could not handle my wife's unfortunate passing with cruelty and still retain all the grandeur the Blackstones enjoy. No, I did indeed make arrangements with her grieving mother and father to have her take a gentle trip back to her home town of Calais. I even sent a priest along with her body."

He spoke with complete callousness and I shuddered. So I was wrong about Lenore's whereabouts, but I was right about one thing. He aimed to kill me. That was why he was reveling in his evil deeds and sharing them with me. A dead woman will tell no tales.

He looked at me with a wild stare. "I see you are horrified. When you arrived, I thought you would be easy to fool or dispose of. It mattered little to me. Women are two-a-penny, after all."

He suddenly stooped down and untied my ankles. "I cannot set you free entirely, for then you might scream and though there is no one to hear you here, it will be a different matter once we get outside."

Pulling me up to my feet, he kept me in a tight hold. I couldn't even kick, for he rushed me out the door of the tower in a hurry. I tried to resist moving but he pushed me hard and with my hands bound, I was helpless.

We stood outside the tower, Blackheart River dark and rushing at a steady flow. There was no strong wind, only a warm breeze that stirred the air. What did this madman mean to do with me? He had murdered his wife and Miss Drake. There was no doubt he intended the same for me. I tried to pull away but he was too strong and held me so tight, I was having trouble breathing.

His breath was close to my ear.

"You must understand that I cannot allow you to live, Miss Stewart, for you know enough to hang me. But I will promise a quick death, for the weeds will drag you down and caress you while your lungs fill with water."

He meant to drown me! I shook my head as I thought I might pass out but I couldn't. While I still breathed I had to fight.

"I will sadly recount the tale of how you drowned out of despair for what little was left for your life. I can explain how you pleaded for me to keep you as part of the staff but that I had no place for you and could not recommend your services."

I was crazy with fear but held on to one glimmer of hope. I knew the Earl did not know that I was an expert and accomplished swimmer. I began swimming like a fish as a child. It might be possible for me to strike away from the boat and regain the shore. A desperate move for certain, for the moon was full and bright and he might be aware of my every move in the water. Still, it was the only chance I had. I wasn't going to go down into the dark waters of Blackheart River without a fight.

Thirty Five

The light from the full moon made the lantern unnecessary and the Earl left it on the ground. He twisted my arms hard, shoving me toward the clumps of willows where the skiff was moored.

My heart leapt with hope thinking I might be able to attempt escape while he loosened his grip to pull the boat into the river, which he could not do with one free hand. Unfortunately, the boat was already launched, attached to the willows by a slip knot which could be loosened by a single pull.

With a brutal push, he tossed me into the boat and climbed in behind me, cast off swiftly and began to row toward the middle of the deep river. If my hands were free, I would have jumped off immediately, but while they remained tied, I stood no chance. I would drown.

The Earl rowed steadily, the boat rocking slightly. We were near the very middle of Blackheart River when he stopped and shipped the oars. Reaching over, he pulled out a narrow dagger from his coat and cut the rope around my wrists. They'd been bound so tight that my hands were numb. I could scarcely feel them. I knew that now was my chance. I had to run up the courage to jump into the dark water below.

But before I could make a move, he grabbed me, pressing my arms to my side, ripped the gag from my mouth and shoved me over the side! I'd had time for only one deep breath before the water closed over my head and I was going down, down into the cold depths of Blackheart River. I had to swim quickly up for air.

Something slimy and snake-like whipped past my face, and fearing I might get too entangled in the weeds that waited hungrily below, I struggled to the surface, praying I'd gotten far enough away from the boat.

I broke the surface and looked around desperately. I was only a few yards from the skiff and with fear tearing at my heart, I struck out for the river bank. I heard a muffled oath and then the splash of oars. The Earl had realized I could swim and could get away. He was coming after me.

I began to swim faster but knew I could not reach the shore before he caught up with me. The boat was quickly behind me and I saw the dark shape of an oar loom over me. I took a deep breath and dived under, hearing the sound of the oar hitting water above me.

My legs were exhausted as was I but I knew I had to keep going. My dress clung to my body and made it even harder to swim with ease. He knew I would tire and eventually drown if he kept at me. But I wasn't going to let him murder me. Not tonight. I had one desperate move left.

The plan was to swim at the boat and attempt to tip him over. I came up the side of the boat and the Earl swung the oar once again, missing me as I went back down and swam to the other side. He suddenly shipped the oar and instead, leaned over to push me and hold me under the water.

But as he reached over, I grasped both his wrists and pulled with all the strength I had left. It was enough to topple him off balance and he fell against the side of the light boat which rocked wildly and dangerously.

With a sudden rush of adrenalin, I frantically transferred my grip to the gunwale, and under the extra pressure the boat heeled over, flinging the Earl into the water!

I was free. I had to make my getaway now. I immediately began to swim for the bank. It seemed so close and within reach. I could not stop now, even though my legs felt like flimsy weeds themselves. I feared that at any moment, the Earl would rise from the water and drag me down to death.

But I reached the river bank, dragging myself upon the wet sand, gasping for air. I looked back but the river lay placid in the moonlight, the upturned skiff floating lonely and still. No splashing water and no sign of the Earl.

I put my hands to my mouth to stifle a scream of horror. The weeds whose very coils had nearly snagged me and dragged me down to the river floor must have taken him. Lord Blackstone had drowned. The dark, somber woods across the river stood like silent sentinels, the only witnesses to the Earl's end.

I was wet, chilled and exhausted. I had faced death and survived. Yet here I stood in the darkness of the river and I could only think that I was responsible for another human being's death, forgetting that he had plotted not only my own murder, but had murdered my beloved Lenore and the evil Miss Drake. No. I vowed I would not mourn for a monster.

There was no further delaying. I had to get back to Blackstone. Victoria could be there already desperately searching for me. I stumbled to my feet and staggered up the bank toward the path up the cliff.

Just as I approached the foot of the path, I saw someone rushing down towards me, torch blazing. Victoria!

"Annalee! Annalee! Dear God."

I stopped, my knees too weak to continue. I thought they might buckle beneath me. But my heart leapt with joy at seeing Victoria running to meet me.

She scooped me up in her strong arms and held me to her, covering my face with soft kisses.

"Dearest Annalee, what in God's name happened? Are you alright? You are soaked to the skin. Why did you leave the castle?"

I could hardly speak, words did not form.

"Please," I struggled, wanting to collapse in her arms. "Please take me home."

Thirty Six

I clung to her but walked on my own without trouble. Several men with lanterns and torches huddled at the castle entrance. I knew none of them.

Victoria bade them wait in the foyer and then carried me into the spacious library, lowering me gently into a large chair. She took a decanter of what looked like brandy from a side table and poured out a glass.

"Drink that. All of it. I can go and fetch you a change of dress."

"No," I said, reaching out for her. "No, not until you have heard what I have to say." My teeth began to chatter. "Besides, this is the only dress I have that is not tattered."

I looked down at the rug on the floor and tried to focus on what I had to say.

"Your brother—the Earl is dead, drowned in the river, where he planned on drowning me." I looked up at Victoria and I saw her mouth go slack in shock. "You are scarcely going to believe..." I paused, realizing I was being selfish thinking only of what happened to me. "What kept you? I worried so that something had happened to you? I should ask how you are."

She shook her head slightly. "Forgive me, my Annalee, I did not intend to be so delayed. Constable Farnsworth of Lustleigh and I squabbled as to whether he had the right or jurisdiction to come and search the Earl's estate. I did what I could to convince him it was indeed a matter of life and death and I gave him all the permission he needed. I was even forced to drag Mrs. Grable, to whom I'd taken the first cup of chocolate, to relate not only her prowess as a local herbalist and medicinal expert, but to testify that there was indeed enough poison from the Belladonna plant in those two cups of chocolate to kill someone. We rode hard to get here as quickly as we could."

She reached out and took my hands, rubbing them gently. It felt warm and comforting.

"Why don't you finish that brandy while I find something, anything, in which you can wrap yourself and then you can tell me everything."

Victoria left the room, only to return moments later with a blanket which she held out to me.

"I'll be back in five minutes. Take off that wet dress." She smiled as she left once again, closing the door behind her.

Despite fumbling with the buttons of my bodice, my fingers still half-numb, I finished, left the wet rumpled dress on the floor where it landed, and wrapped the warm, soft blanket around myself.

There was a soft knock and Victoria entered the room, pulling up another chair beside mine. Her green eyes fastened on me.

"Now, dearest Annalee, please tell me what happened out in that river."

I did not hesitate and spared no detail. Slowly and precisely, I explained everything that occurred from the moment I awoke to the fight for my life with her brother on Blackheart River. I left nothing out and embellished not a word. I had never been a woman who babbled or engaged in useless talk. I stopped at my description of how I looked back toward the river and saw no sign of the Earl. I shook my head.

"Victoria, if I had not struggled with him, the boat would not have tipped over," I said in a low voice. "And he would not have drowned." Inside, Lord help me, I was not very sorry I had done what I did. I prayed she would understand.

Victoria remained still, her gaze still upon me.

"Do not let your heart be heavy, Annalee. You would have drowned yourself instead. My poor darling, what an ordeal you suffered. How could you know my brother could not swim." She ran a finger softly over my cheek.

I was surprised but in a most pleasant manner.

"Then you believe me? I was so afraid that you would not when I have vilified your brother so."

"Do you think that I did not know what a vile man Foster was?" she said bitterly. "I certainly did not think him a murderer, however..." she paused, a strange, dark look in her eyes. "To have murdered two women, dear Lenore..." She stopped, bowed her head and then looked back at me. "And he planned on killing you as well. Ever since our childhood I have disliked my brother and these

197

past years that dislike grew into hate. He was despicable to every woman he knew. He only married Lenore to please Mother. She thought the LaSalle family from Calais a grand match. Too bad they were not as wealthy as mother thought. Foster had not one jot of feelings for Lenore. Once she could not bear children, she was disposable, and I do not question that he planned her death at all. I could tell you things about him that would sicken you, but he is dead so let them be. If it had not been for Lenore, I would have left this infernal place long ago..."

She stopped, smiled, her green eyes watering, and then reached for my hands once again. "And then you came along into my life. I knew for certain I could not leave any time soon."

Physically, I was exhausted and still feeling numb, but inside, I was conflicted and confused. I had lost Lenore, yet a part of me wanted to fall into the arms of Victoria Blackstone and forget everything. Was I a wicked woman for wanting that? Was I going mad? Or perhaps I was unleashing emotions I was too afraid to let loose.

I leaned back in my chair. "What is to be done now? What shall happen to us, to you, to Blackstone Castle?"

"Scandal must be avoided at all cost," Victoria said. "Not for my sake, I draw scandal where I go and my brother paid to have his buried, but I cannot allow my mother to be pulled into such a horrid situation. It could kill her. The Blackstones, even though Foster tried his best to ruin it, have a long and honorable reputation that goes back to pre-Tudor days and these counties depend on our family's good name and graces. I must ask you to be resolute for a short while longer. You will remain here. I shall make all arrangements. And do not fret over my mother. She will not disturb you. I shall take care of everything."

I felt my eyes tear up. I believed her. I believed she would take care of me. I believed she would make the world right again. Somehow. I believed she loved me. Deeply.

Thirty Seven

I can only surmise that I went into shock for several days from the crushing blow I received when the Earl pummeled me from behind that night in the hallway. I can remember only snippets of waking at intervals burning with heat, a throbbing pain in my head and then somehow, I remember Mrs. Patterson was in the room placing cool and wet cloths to my forehead and forcing a cool drink down my throat. I had the sensation of tossing terribly in my bed. Had I been dreaming? Nightmares?

I finally awakened with crystal clear clarity. The fog was gone and I focused on my room.

"There now, Miss, you're a great deal better. How do you feel this morning?"

Mrs. Patterson loomed over me, the sun shining bright upon her from my open window. She pushed me gently back to the pillows.

"There's no call for you to worry yourself. You've been ill with a slight fever these past three days, but you're on the mend now. The Lady Victoria has made certain that you receive the best care."

I frowned and felt weak, lost. I so wished Victoria were here instead of Mrs. Patterson.

"She's been asking after you each day. Lady Victoria has had to take care of all the arrangements. Such a dreadful thing to have happened, but then, you know nothing about it."

I had to be careful what I said. I didn't know how Victoria had managed the whole horrid ordeal. My best bet was to play the innocent as Mrs. Patterson and the others probably believed.

"About what?" I asked.

"His Lordship's death. The morning you were found to be ill we discovered that the Earl was missing, and then one of the grooms came in with the news that the skiff and its oars were floating on the river. Lady Victoria had that part of the river dragged, and there was his Lordship's body held fast in the weeds." Mrs. Patterson's eyes were large with shock. "He must have gone for a row in the moonlight and somehow upset the boat. And him not even knowing how to swim. He shouldn't have been there, I say." She shook her head and lowered her eyes. "What a shock, to be cut off like that in the prime of life."

I wanted to cry. Cry without restraint. But I couldn't.

"What a dreadful tragedy," I said in a mechanical tone. "And so soon after...the Lady Blackstone." My bottom lip quivered, and I wasn't sure I could control the pain in my heart.

Mrs. Patterson patted my blanket. "Well, you are not fit to get out of bed just yet. I shall send Betsy with a bowl of broth to strengthen you, and I'm certain Lady Victoria will be here later to see you."

It was obvious that Victoria had spun a good tale. She had succeeded in covering the trail to a scandal that would have disgraced and ruined the Blackstone name. She was willing to let the dark deeds of her brother drift away into the sands of unwanted memories. It had been obvious that there was no love between brother and sister, only disdain and hate. In a way, they were as empty as I had been.

I leaned my head back upon the pillow and allowed the warmth of the sun and the sound of birds that chirped outside my window to lull me into a light slumber. Victoria would be here soon.

She was officially Lady Victoria Blackstone now, heir to the Blackstone legacy and land. I was certain the title meant little to nothing to Victoria. I didn't even think she wanted Blackstone Castle. But I had been wrong before in my life. I had been wrong about my father. I made the wrong assumption that he cared for his daughter, his own legacy. Yes, I had been wrong before.

I had washed my face and freshened up and dear Mrs. Patterson had found a dress that fit me and wasn't tattered and dirty or torn.

Victoria walked in my room resplendent in a green brocade jacket, white shirt and buff pantaloons. Her burgundy hair spilled across her shoulders and the sun cast sparkles of red in the highlights. Once more, my heart felt aflutter. I had struggled a long time to understand why her presence caused such reaction, especially when my heart had been Lenore's. And here I stood, with nothing behind me, nothing in the future, still wondering why I wondered. Was I afraid of acknowledging strong, pent-up emotions for her? And why? I knew she loved me. More than perhaps Lenore could have, even if she'd been free to do so.

She eyed me with a curious gaze.

"Has the rest caused your tongue to grow cold?" She smiled as she came to me and took both my shoulders. Her gaze lingered. "No harm shall ever come to you, Annalee. I will take care of you and give you all you should ever need or want, if you would only let me."

She leaned in and kissed me softly and quickly on the lips. They tasted sweet and soft as the petals of a new-born rose. Inside, I wanted to melt into her arms, be taken care instead of fending for myself in a ruthless society. I was tired of fighting the world in which my father left me stranded.

When I didn't respond, she pulled me closer, studying me intently with those deep, green eyes.

"What is it you're afraid of, Annalee? I have proven my love for you. I cannot and will not ask for your heart for I know you loved Lenore..." She paused. "As I finally learned and accepted in my time, you must come to understand that Lenore's heart was not hers to give."

I could not look her in the eyes. In my heart, I knew she was right. Lenore never would have been mine. I would have lived forever in the shadows of the Earl, catching a few precious moments here and there with Lenore. Had I wanted my future to be so bleak? I could not have realistically offered anything to Lenore. I could barely keep myself above water. I cast my eyes to the floor, but Victoria took my chin and brought it up so that I was forced to look upon her.

"I will, in time, hope to take your heart for my own, you know that? I would not be a proper Lady if I pushed myself on you now, but give me at least a fighting chance?" She smiled and kissed me again....on the forehead.

She need not have pleaded so passionately. Victoria Blackstone was my salvation. My knight in shining armor. She was right. I was still haunted by Lenore and the passion I shared with her, but how could I deny that Victoria had not always been present in those emotions as well? I wiped away the tears that had surfaced and smiled wide at her.

"Forgive me for being such an ungrateful fool, dear Victoria. You have been with me since our first meeting."

Victoria flung her arms up in jubilant celebration.

"I so prayed you would not rebuff me! Now, we're all packed and ready to go."

I took a step back. Packed? To go where?

"Leaving Blackstone? You made no mention of leaving. Where shall we go?" I was most curious, as I knew I would certainly not live at the Dower House with or without Victoria. Blackstone Castle was now Victoria's home if she wished to have it. Why leave?

"We have a cottage on the outskirts of Bath. It's the Blackstone family retreat of sorts..." She paused and took my arms once again. "Darling, you and I cannot live here after all that has happened. It will be frowned upon and my mother and others will no doubt cause problems for us. Please, trust me."

And I did. I cannot explain why, but a certain peace, a sense of complete abandonment swept over me. I knew that I would be protected with Victoria. That everything she did was for my best interest.

I leaned my head on her shoulders, inhaling the scent of her.

"I will follow where you lead. I know that what you do is always for the good for the both of us."

"It will only be for a short while. We're going far away."

I leaned back to look at her. This woman was full of surprises.

"Please, do not taunt me with piecemeal revelations, Victoria. I cannot stand all these little surprises in spurts."

She beamed as she gazed at me. "We sail to the United States. I've a few things that must be attended to and arrangements made, but it is the only place we can start anew. America is fresh and open and free. We cannot tie ourselves to these old ways."

I wrapped my arms around her neck and kissed her. I shared her passion for travel to America. I had nothing left here except pain and rebuff from a society that thought itself moral but would not accept those who were impoverished or dared to dissent against strict and duplicitous moral codes.

Victoria grabbed my hand and rushed to the door.

"Your bags are already packed and a coach waits outside."

Epilogue

Annalee Stewart, diary entry November 23, Year of Our Lord, 1829

It is hard to believe that today is the seventh year anniversary of our arrival in Connecticut, United States. It all seems so long ago, yet ever so close. My time at Blackstone Castle will always be part of my life, and Lenore still haunts a small part of me. But a very small part that I keep stored away only to replay it when reviewing my life thus far. I am grateful it no longer makes me sad.

Victoria came to America a very wealthy woman and was treated almost as royalty. She became popular with the aristocracy of New England, and I finally was able to enjoy the life that I once had as child and lost along the way. I have Victoria to thank for bringing me back. As a matter of fact, I have Victoria to thank for everything good in my life. We cannot live an open life and must always find unique ways to fend off eligible young men who are desperate to win the hand of such charming and well off young women. Soon we will both be beyond the age where wistful young men are a problem.

We share a love that is both satisfying and passionate. Oh, what passion! I no longer berate myself for not opening my heart to her sooner. No, too many good years have passed to insist on such negative emotions. My world is filled with passion, romance, love and all I could ever hope. Sometimes I look at Victoria, times she is unaware of my gaze and I must restrain myself from interrupting her reading or writing with the suggestion, ah, the urgent request that we adjourn to our private quarters. She would come with me; I know she would, making my self-imposed restraint all the sweeter for its eventual abandon. We love to make our love to one another, to ignite the unspoken smoldering fires within, or to fan the flames of those other words, the ones we whisper, the ones we share only with one another. But sometimes I save my desires, I do not interrupt her and when at last we are abed, I give her what I have saved up for her. She seems always appreciative! She claims to be a woman of enormous good fortune, and she claims I am a woman of exquisite good taste!

It feels good to be winding down some of the work at the Seminary. I know how much Victoria has invested in Miss Beecher's school for women but I decided I wished to spend more time at home. Victoria's investment in the college has been very satisfactory and her relationship with Catharine Beecher is one of mutual admiration. I know that Victoria thought my involvement with the college might keep me occupied, but my interest in horse breeding and racing has grown, and I want to be here and spend more time with Victoria. It does my heart good to see how she was able to bring her love for horses to our new home and create such a profitable venture.

We've received no posts from the Dowager, who threatened to never speak to her daughter when we left and has kept her word. In the years we've been in Connecticut, not a letter has ever arrived. Victoria kept no connections to Blackstone Castle, having been paid her portion of its worth in British pounds. And quite a handsome sum it was.

In anniversary markers, I often find myself drifting to the past. It's unavoidable I suppose. Even after all these years and a blissful existence in America, I am still haunted by the dark, flowing waters of Blackheart River and the taste of fear as I struggled in its deadly embrace. But not today. No, today, I choose to bathe in the rays of contentment and celebration.

There are no more shadows in my heart though I sometimes think I see the face of Lenore on a certain kind of sunny day. She is smiling, she is happy, she has been loved and she is free. And despite the prior trials and tribulations in my life, I have found my Lady Blackstone. I give her all my heart and she gives me hers. Sometimes in life, there is loss along the way, but I have all one can hope for in life: love given and love returned.

Annalee Stewart

Other exciting Gothic Romances by Patty G. Henderson

The Secret of Lighthouse Pointe

Castle of Dark Shadows

Passion for Vengeance
(Award Winner of a 2014 Golden Crown Literary Society Award and Indie B.R.A.G. Medallion)

The Brenda Strange Paranormal Mystery Series

The Burning of Her Sin

Tangled and Dark

The Missing Page

Ximora

All books are available in paperback and eBooks on Amazon, Barnes and Noble or where books are sold.

Patty G. Henderson

Patty G. Henderson is an author, artist and publisher. She loves historical fiction, especially historical mysteries, film and television. She's also a fan of supernatural literature and films, and the author of the Brenda Strange Paranormal Mystery Series as well as three Gothic Historical Romances and several anthologies.

"My passion to write comes from a desire to entertain. Nothing more. I come from a family who loved to tell tales around the dinner table, my grandmother fondest of ghost stories. If I've managed to lure a reader into another place and time, and after they close the book, the story still lingers, then I've done what I love doing as a writer."

"If I succeeded in doing that, I would be very grateful if you took a few minutes to write a review on Amazon for SHADOWS OF THE HEART or any of my books that you should happen across. Reviews can be very helpful, and I absolutely love to read the various insights from satisfied readers. Thank you so very much. Until we meet again..."

www.pattyghenderson.com

Find me on Facebook.....Patty G. Henderson on FB

Printed in Great Britain
by Amazon

35794871R00126